T IS FOR...

A GROVER BEACH TEAM BOOK

ANNA
KATMORE

GENRE: YA/CONTEMPORARY ROMANCE

T is for...
Third book of the
GROVER BEACH TEAM series
Copyright © 2013 by Anna Katmore
All cover art copyright © 2013 by Anna Katmore
All Rights Reserved

First Publication: October 2013

ANNA KATMORE

T is for...

More books by Anna Katmore

Grover Beach Team series

Play With Me

Ryan Hunter

T is for...

Kiss with Cherry Flavor

*

Summer of my Secret Angel

*

Adventures in Neverland

Neverland

Pan's Revenge

ANNA KATMORE

To Annie

The loveliest and best editor of all time!

Thank you for turning my books into something coherent. ;)

CHAPTER 1

"BEING SEVENTEEN IS no fun if you're not partying. And you can't party if you're hiding in this room."

I laughed at my cousin's antics, but inwardly I cringed when she grabbed my wrist and hauled me out of my room and down the hallway through the mansion. Chloe's bright pink nails bit into my skin. The fact that her nails matched the color of her underwear—*always*—made me shudder. I really didn't need to learn that bit of information right after dinner in front of my aunt and uncle, who were kind enough to take me in for the next four months.

Being the daughter of an army general was pretty tough at times, but at least my parents hadn't made me move during the school year this time. Well, not too far into the year, anyway. It was the beginning of November. Early enough to integrate into high school society and make friends before you were called a total outsider. This was always my worst fear when the word *move* had been dropped in conversations in the past.

I snatched my black hoodie from the coat rack in the hallway before Chloe could crush my arm in the door. As I pulled it over my long-sleeved shirt, my cousin gave me an annoyed stare down her pointy nose.

"Why are you always so cold, Sam? This is California. You don't even wear a coat here in the winter."

For someone who had been living in Grover Beach all her life, this might be true. But for the previous eight months, I'd been living in Cairo. Once you learned to cope with the frying heat in Egypt, anything else felt like walking into a fridge.

"Where are we going, anyway?" I asked.

Chloe pushed me into her white car parked in front of the house and didn't answer until she was buckled in behind the steering wheel. "To town. I'm going to introduce you to a few more friends of mine later tonight."

Ugh. More friends of Chloe—meaning more girls who thought the most important thing in the world was the perfect hairstyle. Now didn't that sound like a promising Saturday night...

I leaned back, hugged my legs to my chest, and closed my eyes. A slap from Chloe two seconds later made me jerk around. "What?"

"Take your dirty boots off my seat! That's leather."

I groaned but dropped my feet to the floorboard. It was her car after all and not my parents' Land Rover, in which no one bothered about sand on the seats. In Cairo, there was sand everywhere.

Chloe drove us to a café in town where several cars were parked in a line in front. The name *Charlie's* was spelled in dark blue, flashing cursive letters above the door.

After we parked across the street, I climbed out after her.

"Is this it? Looks nice." The café had a beautiful outside area, but no one sat at the round tables tonight. Faint music from the 1960s or '70s drifted from the inside.

"This is only our first stop. We're going to meet Brin, Kir, and Les here." Chloe whirled around and sent me a warning glare. "Listen, here are the rules for tonight."

"Rules?" She couldn't be serious.

"You only talk to people I talk to, and if I have a drink tonight, you're not telling my parents. Got it?"

Gee! If I had known I'd get the real army drill in Grover Beach, I'd have borrowed a uniform from my dad and worn it for *a fun night out* with my cousin. I rolled my eyes and headed through the door.

The place was even nicer inside. Terracotta stone tiles gave the room a warm touch. An S-shaped bar lined the side wall, and attractive rattan tables and comfortable chairs stood all over the place. It totally replicated a Caribbean ambience. I would know—before Egypt, my dad had been based in Cuba for two years. I fell in love with this café in an instant.

Chloe pushed at my back. "Don't stand in the doorway gaping. Our table is over there."

No gaping. I made a mental note of that and resisted the urge to salute the drill sergeant, who snorted down my neck. At this point, I thoroughly regretted not bolting the door to my room after dinner.

Heading to the back of the café, I looked over my shoulder and quirked my brows. "Seriously, Chloe, take a breath. It's not like the paparazzi are hiding behind those columns, waiting to snap you doing something outrageous."

She opened her mouth to say something, but a deeper voice beat her to it. "Watch out!"

My head snapped around. I jolted to a halt only seconds before I crashed into a waiter with a tray. He raised a protective hand in front of the empty glasses to prevent them from toppling onto the floor.

"Oh boy, I-I'm sorry," I stuttered, and backed away. When I looked up I was staring into eyes that were as blue as the sky over Egypt, set in a face that could easily attract me. I always fell for boyish good looks, especially if said boys came equipped with tousled blond hair like his. Only trouble was, he was glaring at me like I'd broken the damn glasses already. His harsh gaze moved past me and the scowl on his face deepened.

Chloe pushed to the front. "Hello, Anthony."

I had trouble figuring out if she meant to sound flirtatious or arrogant.

"Bring me a martini at my table." She looked at me, tapping a finger to her lips. "And a club soda for my cousin." Under her breath she added, "You're going to drive home tonight."

I felt the urge to laugh, but I feared Chloe would just use that as another reason to rebuke me, so I restrained myself and instead whispered, "I don't think you'll get alcohol in this place." Then I turned to the waiter, Anthony. I wondered if Chloe was going to introduce us.

She didn't. In fact, she stalked right past him, toward a table at the far end of the room, and sat down with three of her

ANNA KATMORE

friends I had met earlier today, adjusting her black minidress.

Great. I was left standing in front of this guy like an idiot, as he tilted his head and regarded me with a questioning look. Since he seemed to be a friend of Chloe's, maybe he was waiting for me to introduce myself? I offered him a smile. "Hi. I'm Samantha Summers."

The guy rolled his eyes. "Just get out of my way."

Oh...

My shoulders slumped as I took a quick step to the side, and he shoved past me. I wasn't easily embarrassed, but right now I knew my face was glowing like a stop sign.

"Another Summers..." he growled—what—disgusted? "Just what we need."

Gone was my last bit of hope for a nice first evening in my new hometown. I clenched my teeth and hurried to Chloe and her friends, keeping my eyes straight ahead, avoiding the curious stares of the kids around me. Sinking into the seat, I lowered my chin.

"What. Was. *That?*" Chloe's high-pitched voice was as pleasant as disinfectant in my eyes.

"What do you mean?" I snarled back.

"Didn't I tell you just a minute ago not to talk to people you're not supposed to?"

"What?" She had obviously lost it. And I wasn't up to taking crap like that after the rebuff I'd just had to stomach. "You talked to him first. What's wrong with you?"

"I talked to him because I had to. He's the busboy. But we're not friends with him or his like."

"Oh my God, Chloe. Do you ever listen to yourself?" I was ready to rise from the table and make the two-mile hike home. Anything that would save me from my cousin's idiocy. My fingers curled around the armrests, but just as I pushed myself up, Anthony stepped up to our table. For some unknown reason, I slumped back into my seat. Maybe it was the menacing look in his eye that prevented me from leaving.

He slid a bottle of Red Bull across the table to Chloe and one for each of her friends, then he sat a glass of sparkling water with a slice of lemon wedged on the rim in front of me.

"What's this?" Chloe snapped, picking up the bottle and shoving it at Anthony. "I asked for a martini, not Red Bull."

Anthony leaned forward, resting his palms on the tabletop, and glared at Chloe. "I don't think any of you are over twenty-one, so it'll be your usual. Take it or leave it, Summers."

When his harsh gaze focused on me, the heat in my cheeks resurfaced. Dammit, could he stop doing that to me? I swallowed against a dry throat then grimaced sheepishly. "I'm the one with the club soda, remember? I'm sure I don't need to be carded for that."

Something appeared on his face that made him look a lot less intimidating. It took me a second to realize it was a set of dimples. Was that a smile? Well it wasn't exactly, but his gaze softened for sure.

Next thing I knew, Chloe reached across the table and knocked my glass over with surprising clumsiness. The gush of water splattered down the length of my camouflage pants.

"What the heck—" I jumped up at the same time as

12   ANNA KATMORE

Anthony jerked back from the table.

"Watch out, busboy," Chloe spat. "Just look at what you did."

The look Anthony cut her then was asking for a rope to strangle her. "Are you crazy? That was you."

Chloe arched a perfectly shaped eyebrow and leaned back in her chair, arms folded under her boobs. Her voice went deathly cold. "I didn't touch anything. You should try taking your eyes off me next time and concentrate on the simple job you have."

Oh wow, this was Freddy Krueger meets Stephen King's *It*. There was some serious enmity floating between them, and I was sure it had nothing to do with *her* being the queen of her own world and *him* just being a simple busboy. Why did I suddenly feel caught in the middle of something personal?

"Tony! Is there a problem?"

I turned to find a tall man behind the bar looking over at us. He wasn't dressed in black pants and a white shirt like Anthony, but sported a blue T-shirt with a black vest over it.

"*No* problem, Charlie," Tony replied through gritted teeth. Then he yanked a dishcloth from his belt and wiped the table. When it was dry, he slung the cloth over his shoulder and cut me a look that was back to annoyed. "Can I bring you anything else that you and your friends can knock over?"

Words caught in my throat, when I actually wanted to scream at him that he shouldn't drag me into this. They weren't my choice of friends, and Chloe—well, she was family and I depended on her in a way I was starting to really hate this evening. But with the prospect of staying in her house for quite a long time, my options were limited.

So I just shook my head, and Tony left without another word.

A pull on my arm made me drop to my seat again. Chloe frowned in a very disapproving manner as she raked a few strands of her very blond bangs out of her eyes. "There's a lot you have to learn if you want to hang out with us, little cousin."

I was only six months younger than her, but I'd been the little cousin for a long time, due to my unfortunate five feet and two tiny inches. It didn't bother me. What really got on my nerves was the strange, bitchy attitude Chloe seemed to have developed since the last time we'd met.

One of the girls—Breena or Brinna, I couldn't remember exactly—giggled and opened her handbag under the table. Everyone took a turn in reaching inside, except me. When I saw what they fished out of it, my eyes widened. "You smuggled alcohol into this place? Are you insane?"

"Shush!" Chloe poured a tiny bottle of vodka into her Red Bull while the others leaned closer and covered her from the view of the bartender. "This is just to get in the right mood. We're going to a real party later."

Okay, that was it. I didn't have a whole lot of options, but I wasn't going to take that shit from Chloe or anyone else. "I don't care where you go, but *we* are going nowhere. I'm outta here. Give me your car keys. I'm sure Christine—"

"Kirsten," the strawberry blond next to Chloe corrected me sharply.

ANNA KATMORE

"—*Kirsten*, or any of the others, can drive you home."

"I don't think so." Chloe laughed, and she sounded really pissed. "You're not driving my car when I'm not with you."

"You dragged me here and you knocked ice water all over my pants. I'm not exactly having the time of my life here. And I'm definitely not going to *walk* to your house. So give me the damn keys." I paused and leaned closer to her. "Or do you want me to drop a note on the kitchen counter for your mom to read tomorrow?" My voice was a warning hiss. "I'm sure she'd love to hear that you're spiking your drinks."

"You wouldn't dare, you little brat!"

"Try me." I held out a hand, giving my cousin the death glare I'd contained all day—since she'd run her hand through my messy layered hair and told me I looked like a walking bush when she and her parents had picked me up from the airport.

With a snort, Chloe fished the keys out of her handbag and dropped them into my palm. As she gritted her teeth, I wondered whether I was going to pay for this later.

Man, tonight sucked.

I straightened and squared my shoulders. Holding my head high, I walked up to the busboy, who'd stopped by a young couple and was chatting with them. From the pocket of my pants, I pulled out a handful of dollars and tossed them on his tray. "Keep the change."

He gave me a cold look. Obviously, I didn't have to say more. I turned on my heel and strode out the door, only then daring to breathe again. I raked my hands through my hair, getting annoyed when it ended at chin-length. I'd thought it would be cool to cut it before I came here, but right now it sucked just like everything else.

Wow, what a start to my new life.

For a minute or two, I sat on the hood of Chloe's car and stared at my wet thighs. The rusty color of my pants had turned into a darker shade of reddish brown. What had possessed Chloe to do that?

Maybe someone should talk to Aunt Pamela about her daughter. Drinking in public places, behaving like an arrogant ass...this was not how I'd known Chloe when we were younger. Then again, I wasn't a tattletale. I'd never give a family member away—however stupid that person might be. But Chloe didn't have to know that.

My thoughts returned to the busboy. I didn't know anything about him, other than his first name, but the way he'd growled "another Summers" made me wonder what bad bit of past he and Chloe shared. Whatever it was, I refused to get in their line of fire. Their fighting wasn't my concern. Right now I needed to focus on what lay in front of me. I had to start a new school on Monday, and without Chloe taking me by the hand and showing me around, it would be as nasty as all the other times I'd had to start over in the past.

Oh, I couldn't wait...

Going back to the place where I inhabited a room on the same floor as my silly cousin didn't appeal to me right now. With the keys dangling from my fingers, I ambled down the street, my mind set on a little window shopping to distract me. But the stores lining the sidewalk were all dark and some also had rolling grilles in front of them. I peeked through the slits but couldn't make out much.

Now if this wasn't like the entire town was determined to shut me out. A long sigh escaped me. Focused on the dark sky, I strolled on, rounded some corners, and abruptly lost my way. With my fabulous sense of direction, I was good like that. It took an hour and a half and some serious cussing at myself to find Chloe's car again. I hurried toward it from the opposite direction than I had started off. A push of the button on the key fob made the headlights flash twice and unlocked the doors.

Voices to my right drew my attention to the entrance of the café. A small group of kids stood outside. The busboy was with them, and also the couple he'd been chatting with when I'd left earlier.

Chewing on my bottom lip, I slowed down and peered at them from the corner of my eye, wondering if I should try to talk to Tony. Since he seemed determined to put me in the same boat as my cousin without knowing me at all, this was a good chance to set things straight. Okay, the thought of Chloe turning scarlet when she found out I was talking to someone I wasn't supposed to, according to her, might have helped sway me to go for it.

I crossed the street. "Tony?"

He turned around, his smile fading the moment he saw me. *Ugh.*

Eyes narrowed, he angled his head and studied me as I drew closer. I knew this look. It spelled: *Just get out of my way.* Uneasiness settled in my stomach. Maybe this wasn't such a good idea after all. My next step was hesitant, but it was too late to back down. Everyone was looking at me.

"I—" I clasped the cuffs of my hoodie, which reached to the middle of my palms. "I just wanted to say sorry. You know, for what happened back in there. With the water and—"

"For you"—he interrupted my stuttering with a drawl—"it's *Anthony*."

He turned back to his friends, and they walked away.

CHAPTER 2

"WELCOME TO GROVER Beach, Sam," I muttered to myself and trudged to Chloe's car. Banging my head on the steering wheel, I wished she had never dragged me out of the house.

It was just my luck that I hadn't paid attention when we'd come to town, so I had no idea which way to go to get to my uncle's house. I drove around for a while, but that still didn't get me home. Of course, Chloe's car came equipped with a navigation system, so eventually I punched in the address and let the female voice direct me to the Summers' palace. I parked the car outside the closed double-door garage. Moments later, I let myself in with Chloe's keys and stashed them under the doormat. I would send her a text in a minute and let her know where to find the keys later.

The guest room I occupied was on the second floor, and the twin windows overlooked the wide garden below. Right now I could see nothing but my frustrated face reflected in the glass when I gazed out.

I kicked my boots into the corner of the room and dropped across the bed. This room was twice as big as my old one back in Cairo, and though it was fully furnished in matching pieces made of cherry wood, it looked rather empty without any personal decorations. I hadn't brought much stuff. Just a suitcase packed with my favorite clothes, which mostly consisted of hoodies and camo pants, and then of course my drawing stuff.

My cell phone lay on my night stand. I reached for it, wanting to talk to someone and get all the sorrow of a miserable first day off my heart. Egypt was ten hours ahead of California. I could call my mom now and probably reach her during breakfast. But then, what would I tell her? That Chloe had mutated into a bitch and that this guy in the café had embarrassed me like hell?

No, my mother would only worry, and I didn't want to trouble my parents. Letting me go was hard enough for them. If I gave my mom a call, I'd have to sound happy, and I just couldn't summon the effort to do that right now. So I only sent a text to Chloe about the keys then put the phone back down.

I decided to draw instead. It always helped soothe me. On the wide desk in front of the window, paper, pencils, and charcoals were scattered all over the place. Before Chloe had hauled me out, I'd started to draw Lucifer, the wild stallion that used to roam the grounds around our house on the outskirts of Cairo. Nobody ever managed to touch him, but for some reason, he'd always come closer to me than to anyone else. My dad used to say it was probably because he felt connected to me. Untamed and stubborn. Or maybe he just liked my hair, which was pitch-black like his.

Whatever it was, I'd enjoyed the animal's presence and sketched it a hundred times back then. But now, the features, muscles, and shadows just wouldn't work out as I wanted. It was

ANNA KATMORE

hard for me to draw from memory. I missed the live model.

At two in the morning, when Chloe finally sneaked into her room and closed the door just a tad too loud, I gave up and went to bed. Closing my eyes, I expected to dream of Lucifer and the wide scenery of the Egyptian desert. But what came up was a boyish face with eyes that scowled when he looked at me. I groaned and rolled over, dragging the comforter over my head. Sure as hell that rude idiot would be the last thing I thought of before falling asleep.

*

Sunday was cool. I didn't see much of Chloe. Apparently, she was used to sleeping in after a late night out. No one cared, least of all me.

In the evening, I packed my school bag and went through all the stuff I needed three times. I didn't want to miss anything. But by Monday morning, I'd already realized I had missed one essential thing. A ride. Chloe had left without me, and without leaving any directions for how to get to the school too.

"Gee, gonna be a *great* start at Grover Beach High." I squeezed my eyes shut and released a frustrated sigh, then I hoisted my backpack onto my shoulders. There was always the possibility of asking Aunt Pamela to drive me, but it would mean giving reasons, and I really wanted to avoid telling her about Chloe's idiocy today.

Instead, I walked down the lane and asked the first person on the street for directions. The old and obviously deaf lady shouted back, "What do you want?"

"Grover Beach High School! Which direction?" I pointed left and right in turn, making a hopeful face.

Now the woman smiled. "Ah." She pointed her walking stick to the left. "It's two miles that way," she screeched so loudly I wondered if she thought me as deaf as herself.

If I wanted to be at school before the bell rang for the first class, I had to run. Two yolk-yellow buses passed me as I jogged down the street. At least now I knew when to catch one tomorrow.

Sweating and panting, I arrived at the building within fifteen minutes. And I still had enough time to look for the office and get my schedule.

Mrs. Shuster, the secretary, was already expecting me as I opened the opaque glass door and stepped into the office. I had spoken to her on the phone the previous week, letting her know which classes I intended to take apart from the four core subjects, English, math, science, and U.S. history. I'd picked journalism, PE, and then of course, art.

Mrs. Shuster had told me about a special class they offered, which was called Animation & Visual Effects. I had been in a similar advanced class back in Cairo and couldn't wait to continue my studies here. Gifted with calm hands and an eye for detail, my goal was to work for Disney Pixar one day. Either that or I'd become a professional dancer. I loved to move almost as much as I loved to draw.

The secretary had me sign a few forms, then she handed me my class schedule and a map of the school building. With that many corridors, it would be a miracle if I ever found my way back out.

I tracked my way to science with my finger on the map, looking up every now and then, checking that I was still on the right path. One last left turn and...*ta da!* Lifting my chin, I stared at a closed door that had the image of a stick man on it. The sound of flushing toilets and running faucets drifted out. This was most probably *not* the science classroom.

I checked the map again. Where the heck had I taken a wrong turn?

The door suddenly swung open and, with the large paper clasped in both hands, I gaped up into a boy's face. Before I even knew why, my heart lurched to my throat.

Tony stopped dead before he ran me over. He made an effort to look *down* on me, as if my short height annoyed him above all else.

Oh, come on, it wasn't really that bad. If nothing else, my height was just cute. He could probably rest his chin on the top of my head if he hugged me.

Wait. I didn't just think *hug*, did I? Definitely not with this ass, no way.

"You're going to school here?" he asked me then, and by the sound of it, that was surely the worst thing that could happen to him.

"Umm...y-yeah." Dammit, I hated my recent habit of stuttering. This wasn't me. Well, not the normal me, anyway. I cleared my throat and straightened my spine, which gave me the final inch I needed to find my self-confidence again. "First day."

Tony's gaze dropped to the map in my hands, then moved back to my face. His expression changed to one of amusement as he arched one brow. "Taking your first class in the men's room?" He gave me no time for a comeback but carefully shoved me to the side with the back of his arm and walked away.

I stuck my tongue out after him which he really couldn't see. Then I banged the back of my head against the wall and immediately regretted it as the pain vibrated through my skull.

Okay, starting again. I located the men's restroom on the map, then worked my way from there to the science classroom. This time I found the way and slumped, relieved, into a seat at the back of the room.

A bunch of students filed in at the ring of the bell. One very tall guy wearing a black sweatshirt with the hood pulled up over his head walked toward me and then stopped, giving me a strange look. The slim cable from iPod headphones ran down the length of his neck, and a few strands of red hair flashed from underneath the hem of his hood. "Move over," he growled. "That's my seat."

"Good morning to you, too," I mumbled, but I didn't think he could hear me with the headphones plugged into his ears. I scooted to the seat next to him, sliding my books along with me. He didn't send me away, so I might've had to sit next to an unfriendly giant, but at least I got to sit *somewhere*.

A female teacher walked in behind the last couple of kids. Her hair was dyed a brilliant white and funky green glasses sat on her pert nose. She looked around the room until her gaze landed on me. Smiling, she motioned with her hand that I should come forward.

I knew this was going to happen, but a shudder slithered down my spine at the thought of the formal introduction nonetheless. At least I'd only have to do this seven times today, and then the horror would be over.

Mrs. Hallshaw, that was her name, made me stand in front of the class and tell everyone where I came from and what I liked to do.

I shoved my hands into my pockets. "My name is Samantha Summers, but please call me Sam. My dad's a general in the U.S. Army. He opted for out-of-country work, so that's why I've been to nine different schools already." Rocking back on my heels, I leaned against the blackboard. "In nine different countries."

Some of the faces in the crowd took on intrigued expressions. One of the guys in the back even whistled through his teeth.

"Awesome," said a girl, her eyes widening behind her glasses. If she knew the bad side of it, which mostly concerned the non-existent social life of that general's daughter, she probably wouldn't have said that.

"Try memorizing nine different city maps, nine maps of high schools, and learning four different languages just to be able to order the right sort of spaghetti in a restaurant," I told her, exhaling a sad breath. "It's not that much fun really. And just when you figure out where to buy cool clothes in that new town, your parents tell you sorry, but you have to move again."

The girl with the glasses pulled a face. "Ouch. That sucks."

"You speak four languages?" the teacher asked, and I turned to look at her impressed face.

"Yes, ma'am. English, Portuguese, Finnish, and a little Arabic." In fact, my Arabic was limited to the basic terms of greeting and asking for the price, but it was enough to get me through eight months in Cairo. I was lucky. Most people spoke English there, and even the school I had gone to was a private one for American kids.

"Can you say something in Finnish?" another girl with pigtails asked. She looked slightly familiar. I wondered if I had seen her somewhere in the café Saturday night.

"Rakastan piirtämistä ja tanssimista," I pulled from the top of my head for her.

Some of the kids laughed at the clearly foreign sound of it, but all of them seemed super impressed.

"What did you say?" Spectacle Girl demanded and pushed her wavy brown hair behind her shoulder.

"She loves to draw and dance." The answer came from the tall guy with the hood and the iPod. His lips were pressed together, but he smiled. He had me completely gawking at him open-mouthed.

After Mrs. Hallshaw dismissed me and I walked back to my seat, the tall guy turned to me and pulled down his hood. No longer disguised, he actually looked cute. He held out one hand. "Hi. I'm Niklas Frederickson. You can call me Nick."

"Hi, Nick." I wanted to say something cool, but I only stared at him for a second, then I asked, "Are you from Finland?"

ANNA KATMORE

"Sweden, actually. But I lived in Finland for a few years before we moved to California."

"Cool." And I really meant it. "How long have you been living here?"

"Six years. So...you love to dance? What do you do?"

"A bit of everything. Ballet, hip-hop, funk, breakdance." I grinned, knowing this sounded like I couldn't get my shit together and stick with just one style. "I'm enthusiastic."

He gazed at me with narrowed eyes, as if he was deliberating something. "Sounds good. You should speak to Alyssa Silverman. She's a friend of mine and captain of the cheerleading team. I know she's looking for new members."

"Wow." A cheerleader. I laughed. "I know I just said enthusiastic, but I don't think I'm that type of girl." Mostly because I was short and didn't have the hairstyle for it: long, blond, and perfect. Now I was wondering if Chloe was a cheerleader.

Mrs. Hallshaw cleared her throat, and Nick and I fell silent for fifteen minutes. But when we had to do a partner experiment on some dead fish, he gave me a small piece of paper with a number scribbled on it. "This is Allie's number. If you want to check out the team, give her a call."

"Okay...thanks." I tucked the note into my pocket. "I'm surprised there's cheerleading here at all. Does Grover Beach even have a football team?"

"We don't. But we play soccer at this school."

I had watched exactly one half of a soccer game in Finland. Not my kind of sport, really. "You play?"

"Yep. I'm a Grover Beach Bay Shark." He gave me a smile, revealing that one of his front teeth was chipped. Maybe a soccer accident. I tried not to stare at it, but it was hard when he didn't stop smiling.

"So, um, what position do you play? Quarterback? Pitcher?"

Nick angled his head as though he was trying to figure out what language I was currently speaking. "Quarterbacks are in football. And we sure as heck don't have a pitcher. I'm the goalie."

"Oh." So he'd probably stopped a ball with his face once or twice, thus the chipped tooth. I resisted asking about it and instead pushed the plate with the fish toward him to let him do the dissecting. "I can't handle dead animals. They give me chills." Even now a shiver made my hair stand on end.

Nick had no problems with the dead fish. He sliced into it like it was a warm biscuit.

After science, I battled my way through the crowded corridor to U.S. history, and then further on to English, where I found a seat next to the girl from science class with the wavy brown hair and glasses. Her name was Susan Miller, and she turned out to be really funny. We had to write a poem about any fruit we liked, and she titled hers "Ode to My Banana". I'd just taken a sip from my Coke while she was reading out the poem, and when everyone barked with laughter, I snorted Coke through my nose. Yeah, I could be so attractive when I wanted to be.

Susan also had math with me, and since she'd heard my introduction three times today, she took it into her hands to introduce me to two of her friends before fifth period: Simone Simpkins, who looked like a Norwegian model in super-tight clothes and with perfect blond curls, and Lisa Matthews. Both girls seemed very nice, even though Lisa didn't say much. She seemed to study me for a really long time. Awkward. The fact that she was part of the couple Tony had talked to in the café on Saturday made me doubly uncomfortable.

"You're Chloe Summers' cousin, aren't you?" she finally said, tying her long brown hair up in a high ponytail.

"Um, yeah. Is that a problem?" After the incident with the busboy, I wasn't sure.

"Seriously? Chloesetta is your cousin?" Susan blurted and shoved her metal-rimmed spectacles farther up her nose. "I would have never guessed that. You're so...down to earth."

Everyone laughed. Me the loudest. Most of all because she'd called my cousin Chloesetta and I had no idea why. "Yeah, she's a little...eccentric. I'm living with her and her family until my parents move back to the States in four months. I don't remember her being that snobbish from when we were younger."

"She's like—the Barbie clone," Simone said, then pointed a thumb at Lisa. "Her words, not mine. But she does have a rep at this school, and not a very nice one, if you get what I mean. Thus why some of the kids started to call her Chloesetta. She's known to drag boys into her closet all the time."

Oh, I totally understood. Took me only five minutes with Chloe to figure that out.

After journalism, the three girls pulled me along into the

cafeteria. It was nice to have someone I could sit with during lunch break. Normally, it took me a few days to make friends at new schools. Today was different. I really enjoyed the girls' company. And in the cafeteria, I also saw Nick again. He sat at a long table with a few other athletic guys. His ginger hair stood out from them all. I waved at him as we passed them, and he smiled.

"You know Frederickson?" Lisa said into my ear as we lined up to get our lunch.

"Yeah. Finnish broke the ice." I grinned at her over my shoulder, then picked out a thin slice of pizza, table water, and a cherry lollipop.

Simone grabbed half a pizza, and Susan and Lisa each got themselves a hamburger with fries. I followed them through the room, wondering where we'd sit. My mouth fell open when we steered toward the table with the hunky guys, but I closed it quickly.

"Hey, Finn Girl," Nick said and pulled out the chair next to him with his right foot for me. "How's your first day going?"

I set my tray down and lowered into the pink vinyl chair. "Better than expected." I smiled then bit the corner of my pizza.

He stared from his loaded tray at my lollipop. "Is that all you're going to eat?"

"She's short. She doesn't need as much as you, Frederickson," someone said behind me. The layer of ice in that voice made me hunch my shoulders, and the pizza got stuck in my throat. I didn't need to look back to know who it was.

Tony walked around the table and slumped into the seat

ANNA KATMORE

between Lisa and Simone, then he leaned in to Lisa with his cold eyes on me. "And why's *she* sitting with us?" A moment later, he grimaced. "Ouch!"

Lisa scowled at him. "That was for being an idiot."

He flashed his teeth at her in the parody of a smile. At the same time, the tall, black-haired boy I had seen with Lisa in the café came up behind her. He pulled playfully on her ponytail, leaned down, and pressed a kiss on her neck. "Why are you kicking my best player, Matthews?"

Player? Did they all play soccer like Nick?

Lisa briefly closed her eyes and smiled, obviously enjoying the caress. Hot damn, who wouldn't? The guy was sexy as hell. "Because he deserved it," she replied when he swung his leg over the backrest of the seat on her other side and sat down.

"Hey, what's your problem, Tony?" Nick chuckled around a mouthful of fries, then shoved more of them in his face.

Tony met my gaze across the table. I wondered if he'd rather sit in a different corner of the room right now. Just why did he hate me? It wasn't like I had *leper* tattooed on my forehead or something.

With a sigh, I put my pizza down, having lost my appetite. I wiped my fingers on the white paper napkin. "The problem is that I'm Chloe Summers' cousin." Whatever that meant to Tony.

All the boys at the table stared at me for a couple of seconds. Even Nick glanced at me sideways. "Oh. Is that so?"

I nodded.

"You don't look like her."

Now I laughed, glad I hadn't just sipped from my drink.

Spilling water through my nose in front of them all was the last thing I wanted. "Yeah, we're not made from the same sperm, you know," I told Nick, rolling my eyes and shoving his shoulder.

"But Sam's going to live with Chloe's family," Simone stated with a sympathetic look as she fed a grape to a guy with a blond mohawk next to her. "In the same house for four months."

"Ooh, that's bad," said the boy who'd kissed Lisa's throat, not looking up from picking the pickles out of his cheeseburger. "Hey, Alex, pass the ketchup."

Simone's boyfriend sent the bottle skating across the table to our end, but another burly guy caught it and started pouring the mess all over his spaghetti.

"Ew, Sasha, leave some in the bottle, would you?" Lisa wrestled the ketchup from his hands and gave it to her boyfriend, who squeezed the rest of the sauce onto his burger.

A moment later, Nick made me jump in my seat when he shouted, "Hey, Al, get your sexy ass over here for a sec!" I tracked his gaze across the room to a slim, tall girl with hair as black as mine, only it reached to the waistband of her pair of bell-bottoms and not just to her chin.

She put her tray down at a table surrounded only by girls, then headed over to us. "Hi, guys, what's up?"

"Are you still looking for members for your team?" Nick asked.

Ugh. A cheerleader. I clamped down on my molars, wishing he wouldn't do this right now. One glance at me and the girl would decide that cheerleading and I were not compatible.

"Yes. We finally convinced Lisa to join us, but we're still short of two. Know anyone?"

It was so funny how suddenly both boys to the left and right of Lisa looked at her with dropping chins. The tall one with the black hair flashed a half-smile, mouthing, "You did?"

"I only said that I'd check out the training," Lisa defended herself quickly. Then she grinned cynically over her shoulder. "Thank you, Allie."

"Oh, you're so going to cheer for me, baby." Her boyfriend nibbled at her ear.

Lisa shoved him away like a cuddly puppy and laughed. "Go eat your burger, Hunter."

Nick rested his arm on the backrest of my chair. "Al, this is Sam Summers. She just moved back to the States, and I hear she's good at dancing."

Alyssa Silverman smiled, leaned over the table, and held her hand out to me. Her long hair fell forward and almost into Tony's food. He brushed it aside and back over her shoulder, then he gave Nick a death glare, which Nick didn't notice, because he was looking at me. Yeah, Tony could make you feel totally welcome, whatever you did.

"Nice to meet you, Sam," Al said as we shook hands. "What kind of dance?"

"Um, a mix, really. I'm a little into everything."

"Sounds cool. If you're interested, we can take a look at what you can do. I have PE next period. Any chance you'll be there?"

I quickly recalled the schedule I got from Mrs. Shuster this morning and nodded.

"Fantastic. See you guys later." She waved and hurried back to her friends.

Oh wow. This was new. I'd totally expected her to embarrass me in front of them all with some off comments about my unruly appearance. But she seemed cool with it.

"This is awesome," Susan giggled and clapped her hands. "Lisa and Sam will both be cheering for us."

"I don't see what's cool about that," Tony muttered, and I knew he meant me.

I decided to ignore him for now and instead raised my brows at Susan. "For us? Don't tell me *you* play soccer!"

"Co-ed team," Lisa explained. "Your cousin is on the team, too. Didn't you know?"

"I haven't talked to her much since I got here. So, no, I didn't know. And that's totally crazy. My cousin...playing soccer." I shook my head. "Are we really talking about *Sorry-I-can't-type-on-a-keyboard-because-I-could-break-a-nail* Chloe?"

Oh my God, what was that? Did Mr. Cold and Furious actually let a smile slip? Well, if he did, he was fast to bite it down.

"Yeah," Hunter said. "And she's really good, too."

Now Lisa lowered her chin and cast him an annoyed look. I wondered if she was unhappy about that fact. Maybe I could ask her about it later. And then some more about Tony, too.

While everyone was eating their meals, I ignored my pizza,

unwrapped my lollipop, and stuck it in my mouth. The cherry taste unfolded on my tongue as I sucked it hard. *Delicious*. I sighed.

When Susan quirked her brows at me behind her glasses, I pulled the sucker out with a smack and pointed it at her. "These are the best things in the world. I haven't had one in eight months." I stuffed it back in my mouth and rolled it into one cheek with my tongue. "Mmh, so good. I could live on them and nothing else for the rest of my life."

"She's like you with your cheese crackers," Lisa said and elbowed Tony playfully in the ribs. "Only she doesn't put mayo on the sucker."

Mayo on a lollipop? What was she talking about?

Tony gave Lisa a look equally as cold as he'd given me when he'd joined us. "She's not like me. Most of all because she's short. And that's also why she shouldn't be on the cheerleading team."

His chair scraped on the linoleum floor as he rose and carried his tray away. Moments later, the double doors swung closed behind him.

CHAPTER 3

"I DON'T GET it. What did I ever do to him?" I slumped down on the low bench in the locker room and kicked off my boots.

A compassionate expression on her face, Lisa said, "Don't mind Tony." She started to unbutton her jeans and pulled her gray Mickey Mouse sweatshirt over her head. "He's just a little allergic to the name Summers right now."

"Yeah, I figured that out. So what's the big deal? What's Chloe got to do with him?"

Lisa's mouth quirked to one side. "Simply put, he liked her, then he slept with her last summer, and she dumped him the same night."

"Holy shit!" He had been with my cousin? My eyes were probably wider than saucers right now. Had Tony been in love with Chloe? That was hard to believe after the way I'd seen him talk to her. He had been stone cold, without any affection—just like he was around me.

Lost in a daze, I saw Lisa angling her head. "Are you okay?" she asked.

"Sure." I cleared my throat. "I just didn't think Chloe would turn into that sort of bitch. Now I understand why he doesn't like to hear our last name."

ANNA KATMORE

"Yeah, but there's more to the story," Simone chipped in and snaked an arm around Lisa's shoulders. The girls looked at each other, then Simone started to grin. "Right?"

Lisa sighed, and that was when Susan took over. She really loved to talk. "The thing is Lisa was in love with Tony like forever. But he didn't notice. Or maybe he did, and he just didn't have the guts to tell her he loved her, too."

So he had been in love with Chloe *and* Lisa? The thought of it gave my chest a funny squeeze. Well no, it wasn't funny. Strangely enough, it felt annoying. I didn't want to be the only person in the world he hated.

"But one day," Susan went on, taking no notice of my sudden unease, "Ryan Hunter came along and stole Lisa from Tony."

Lisa laughed. "He didn't steal me." She glanced my way. "Didn't have to. I went of my own free will."

"Yeah right, after the two guys fought over her." Simone made an awed face. "In her bedroom."

Tony got in a fight over Lisa? She did seem nice enough to have guys lining up for her, and she was beautiful, too, in a very natural way. Suddenly, I envied her a little. If I hadn't cut my hair and looked a little more like her, Tony might find me attractive, and then he wouldn't be such an ass around me. Boys didn't behave like jerks around the girls they found pretty. Right?

But why in the world would I even bother? He was just one stupid boy getting on my nerves. I could ignore him. It shouldn't be too hard.

I slipped into my sneakers and tied the laces, looking up at Lisa. "Ryan Hunter is the guy from lunch, right? So he got you, and Tony is pissed?"

"Nah, he isn't pissed." Lisa slipped into a white tee, and so did I. When her head emerged from the collar, she said, "Tony's cool with how things are. We're still best friends."

"Only he doesn't get to sleep in your bed anymore." Simone snickered. When Lisa swatted her on the shoulder, Simone skipped off with Susan behind her.

As we followed, I asked with a strange edge to my voice, "Tony used to sleep in your bed?"

"Yep. For years. We did everything together. It was just so normal for us."

"Did you kiss him?" I bit my tongue. Dammit, I didn't want to ask that, and I wasn't even interested in the answer, so why the hell did it slip out?

"No, not really. He kissed me. Last summer. But only once, after I'd fallen for Ryan. Why do you ask?" Lisa paused and flashed a Peppermint Patty smile. "Are you interested in Tony?"

"God, no!" And that was that. I strode a little faster into the gym and hurried over to Simone and Susan, who were chatting with Allie by a pair of gymnastic rings.

All three grinned at me as I approached them. That gave me an eerie chill. "Up to something?" I asked. Yeah, they definitely were.

"Simone just pointed out your perfect height," Susan explained.

"My perfect height?" My voice had gone dry. No one had

ever put it like *that*. And the fact that these girls had, made me very uncomfortable. "Perfect for what?"

Allie stepped forward and placed a hand on my shoulder. "You know how cheerleaders do those choreographies where they toss a girl in the air and catch her again?"

"Nuh-uh. No way!" I slipped away from her. "You're not going to throw me in the air like a bouncy ball. You can throw Simone. She looks like she'd enjoy that."

"Simone is a good dancer, but she's a coward," Allie said and immediately got a shove on the shoulder.

"I'm not a coward," Simone blurted out. "I just don't trust you guys!"

"Oh, great. But I should?" They had to be kidding me. "And why don't you trust them, anyway? Don't you do this all the time?"

Allie rubbed the back of her neck, wrinkling her nose. "What exactly did Nick tell you about our team?"

"He didn't say anything. Just that you're cheering for the soccer boys. And girls," I quickly corrected after a glance at Susan, who wasn't wearing her glasses for once. "Why? Is there something wrong with your team?"

"No. We're cool. We're just not professionals is all."

"What do you mean?"

"We sort of thought it would be fun to cheer for our boyfriends," Simone chipped in. "At soccer, you don't normally have cheerleaders, but the guys liked it when we came to their games and did some amateur dancing during halftime. So we watched some really cool cheerleading movies and tried to copy their moves." She jumped and threw her left leg in the air, waving her hands like she was holding pompoms.

Lisa cast Simone a mocking grin. "You want me to do *that*, too?"

"Yeah, throw your leg up, Matthews. I'm sure Hunter wants to know what you're wearing under your skirt when you dance."

"Hunter will find out after practice."

Everyone laughed at that. Only I pulled a quizzical face. "Um, is there a deeper meaning to why you call your boyfriend by his last name all the time?"

Lisa shrugged. "He started it."

"Yeah, he never calls her Lisa," Susan told me.

"Never?"

"No. When he doesn't call her Matthews, he calls her...*baby*." At the last word she lowered her voice to sound really deep and grumbling. Too funny. I slapped my thigh as I laughed out loud.

The girls had said they cheered for their boyfriends, so now I got curious. "Who are you with?" I asked Allie when I had calmed down.

"She's with no one," Simone told me. "Yet. But she's working really hard on Sasha Torres. You saw him at our table at lunch."

"The one with the short brown hair? Really?" Oh my God. Did she know how he ate his spaghetti? I guessed not, or else she might have reconsidered. Or maybe not. He was hot, like most of them.

Allie flushed a sensational pink. Heck, she *was* working on him.

"Does he like you, too?"

She shrugged one shoulder, but a smile crept onto her pretty face. "I hope so." Then she cleared her throat. "Anyway, we should see what you're capable of before Miss Trent blows her whistle."

Looking in the direction she did, I saw a middle-aged woman in sportswear marching into the gym and straight for the equipment closet. She held a small silver whistle between her teeth but didn't blow it.

"Okay," I said. "What do you want to see?"

"Can you do backflips? That would be so cool," Susan blurted.

Actually, I couldn't. But from my ballet lessons I had gleaned some severe agility. To show off, I bent backward until I touched the floor behind my heels, then moved my weight onto my arms and lifted my legs over one after the other in a cartwheel motion to stand upright again.

Their mouths sagged open. I grinned. They sure hadn't expected that. Susan pulled on her hair, her eyes really wide. "Shit, that was amazing."

Allie nodded. "I say, if you have just a hint of rhythm, too, you're in."

"Cool." I didn't know if I should be happy now or go find a toilet and flush myself. Then again, any dancing had to be better than no dancing, so I tried to smile.

"We'll do some choreo tomorrow afternoon," Allie told me.

"Come to the soccer field after school, then you can meet the rest of our team and decide if you want to join."

"Okay. As long as I don't have to date a player to be accepted, I'll come."

Susan laughed and looped her arm around mine. "I can be your date." She had adopted that deep, rumbling voice again and dragged me to the rest of the students who'd started doing some warm-up stretching.

Miss Trent let us choose a game for today's sports lesson. Thank God everyone wanted to play volleyball, the only ball game I was any good at. After class, I got my things together and hurried back to the main building to find the room where I was supposed to have my last lesson, Animation & Visual Effects. I had been looking forward to this period all day.

With the ring of the bell, I slipped through the door and slid into the empty seat closest to the teacher. It was a woman in her late thirties wearing a nice floral dress and heeled sandals that clacked on the floor as she walked over to me. "You must be Samantha Summers. Welcome to AVE," she said in a low voice, and we shook hands. "I'm Caroline Jackson. I assume Mrs. Shuster told you what to bring to this class?"

I nodded and opened my portfolio of sketches that I had drawn during the past week. "I have the charcoal portrait of an old woman and the animated antagonist. What troubled me a little was the baby in motion, because we don't have any babies in our family. I prefer to draw from live models. But I found something on YouTube to work with."

"You're inventive. That's good." Mrs. Jackson studied each

ANNA KATMORE

of my drawings for a few seconds. "Your pictures are quite professional. I wasn't sure what to expect when I heard a new student would be joining, but now I see you definitely have talent and belong in this class." She cast me an approving look. "At the beginning of each lesson, I like to discuss the projects of two or three students with the rest. I'd like to start with yours today, if that's fine with you."

I nodded but immediately tension knotted my stomach. I knew I could draw. I just didn't know how good the others were and where I fitted in with my talent. Then again, Mrs. Jackson seemed pleased with my sketches, so I breathed deeply and forced myself to calm down while she clipped them on the whiteboard.

The class began analyzing my *Baby in Motion* first. There was really not much they critiqued. They liked the *Portrait of an Old Lady* even better and pointed out that I had done a fantastic job with the wrinkles and deep lines around her eyes. That was when I finally relaxed in my chair. I had passed their critical examination. *Phew.*

Finally, Mrs. Jackson moved to my last piece, *The Animated Antagonist.* It was a three-layered sketch of a spaceship captain, who was swinging around with a lightsaber in his hand and shoving his dark-purple cape back over his shoulder. To my eyes, it was perfect. I'd worked for ten hours on this particular move. Everyone seemed impressed, which put a beaming smile on my face.

Until a low mumble from the back of the classroom pulled me out of my euphoria. "God. What a baby face."

The suppressed laughter of a few guys followed. The hairs on my arms rose. I didn't want to turn around, but I felt my upper body slowly twist in my seat nonetheless. My gaze fell on the cold eyes of Anthony sitting in the last row of the room.

"Mr. Mitchell, is there anything relevant you want to add about this work?" Mrs. Jackson said loudly.

He tapped his lips with his forefinger, deliberating for a couple of seconds, then said, "Actually, yes." In his voice, I clearly caught his delight at getting the chance to rip me to pieces through my work.

I wrapped my arms around myself.

"While the motion of the antagonist and the balanced composure, as well as the hunky body, may work with a bad-guy image, the artist totally messed up the facial expression. She clearly has an obsession with dimples, which we already got to see in pictures one and two, and the baby-blue eyes of this antihero should have been sketched in a meaner, more furious way. Samantha Summers' antagonist may scare the shit out of Winnie the Pooh, but that's it, I'm afraid."

The entire class burst out laughing. I wanted to cry. My face burned like I'd been left in the sun for ten hours.

Mrs. Jackson pulled my sketches off the board and handed them to me. "Thank you very much for your assessment, Mr. Mitchell," she said in a sarcastic tone. "Why don't we look at your work next?"

"Sure." Tony grinned and winked at me as he sauntered to the front. It wasn't a nice gesture, but utterly cold and mean. He knew he'd hurt me. And the ass was enjoying it.

Why?

He couldn't really be so cruel as to be doing it just because Chloe knocked that glass over Saturday night. He had to know I wasn't impressed with her antics and that I certainly didn't want to get him into trouble with anyone. Why was he so blind? And stubborn? *Goddammit!*

Tony tacked his drawings onto the whiteboard with big, round magnets.

My thoughts got knocked to the wayside and my mouth fell open. He hadn't caught the baby's side view like I had. Instead, the tiny thing was crawling toward the viewer in a way that made one want to reach out and pick it up. And *his* antagonist was a brutal knight on a mean black horse. With a greedy expression, the knight gave the animal the spurs a little more on each layer, making it rise on its hind legs. Fantastic work.

But it was the third drawing that really took my breath away. I didn't know who that woman was, but it could have been the lovely grandmother of anyone. Her face showed the scars of a long, hard life. And even if her lips were thin and straight, her happiness and hardship—it all shone through her eyes.

It was perfect.

I kept silent while some of the others commented on the precise charcoal strokes and the accurate use of light and shadow. No one shredded Tony's confidence like he had done with mine. I lowered my face so he wouldn't spot my awe as he grabbed his pictures and returned to his seat.

During the rest of the lesson, I concentrated hard on what

Mrs. Jackson told us, so I wasn't tempted to brood over Tony's latest act of cruelty against me. But frankly, my heart was bleeding. If any other person had said shit like that about my drawings, I wouldn't have thought twice about it. But after seeing what a great talent this guy had, it meant something. Maybe he was right. Maybe I'd messed up the project with the antagonist. I would have to try harder on the projects to follow and not give him the slightest reason to get at me like that ever again.

After AVE, as everyone got their things together, Mrs. Jackson called me to her desk. "There is a goal I want each of my students to meet at the end of this semester. Since you've missed a couple of months already, you need to catch up with at least the most important projects. About five completed pieces of work. Do you think you can handle that within a couple of weeks?"

"Um, sure." I stepped to the side to let a bunch of kids pass behind me. "What do I have to do?"

She smiled briefly then shouted over my shoulder, "Tony! Please wait a moment."

The shudder his name ignited within me intensified when I turned around and saw him coming toward us.

"What's up?" He cut a brief look down at me, then back at our teacher.

Instinctively, I took a small step away from him and pinned my eyes on Mrs. Jackson with rising horror.

"Could you give Miss Summers your notes on the main projects and explain what she has to do?" Mrs. Jackson asked

ANNA KATMORE

him.

"Heck, no!" Tony raised his eyes to the ceiling and let out a disbelieving laugh. I wanted to do the same at her ridiculous suggestion.

Mrs. Jackson lifted her brows. "Excuse me?"

"Come on, Carrie. This is so cliché. You're only doing this because you're mad about my honesty from earlier."

"That wasn't honest, it was unnecessary. And it's not the reason I want you to help Miss Summers."

Despite the weirdness of this discussion, all I could think was: wow, he got to call her by her first name without being told off.

"No?" he grunted. "Then why?"

"Because you're my best student, and there's no one more qualified to help her than you." She smiled, and I thought it held a hint of mockery. But that couldn't be. Not between a teacher and her student. And she needed to stop talking right this minute. I didn't want this guy helping me with anything.

"I don't care," he snapped. "I don't want to give her my notes."

Mrs. Jackson sighed. "Fine. Then would you please send Jeremy back inside. I'll ask him to share his notes with Miss Summers."

Yeah. Get Jeremy. I'd rather have his notes.

But Tony didn't leave. He folded his arms over his chest and leaned a few inches back. "Seriously? You want to pair her up with Jerry? The guy can't do a stick figure for a bathroom stall."

I don't care. Go get him!

"He's almost as good as you," Mrs. Jackson countered.

"No way." Tony barked a laugh. "I can't believe you'd resort to using *him*."

Wow, had she actually hurt his pride? I had to bite down a smile, even though the situation was not amusing.

"Unfortunately, you give me no choice," she said.

"She won't even be able to decode his notes. Have you ever seen them?"

Mrs. Jackson grinned, but not at Tony. She grinned at me. Something funny was going on in her head, a plan only she knew about. And judging by her smile, it was working. I wished it wasn't.

Tony growled as he dropped his backpack between his feet, leaned over, ripped a yellow Post-it from a stack on the desk, and scribbled something on it. He handed me the note, looking more annoyed than ever. "I have soccer practice today but I'll be home after four. You come. You get my notes. You leave. I'm sure you're a smart girl and can figure out the rest by yourself."

I should have told him what he could do with his *charming* offer but, totally dumbstruck, I just stared at the little yellow note in my hand instead.

Tony hoisted his backpack over his shoulder and gave the teacher a hard glare. "Your psycho shit sucks."

"I love you, too, dear nephew," she cooed after him as he strode out the door.

CHAPTER 4

OMG, I HAD a date...with the biggest jerk in town!

I rolled my eyes. This was so not going to happen. He didn't like me, he didn't want to have anything to do with me, and the feeling was totally mutual. I scrunched up the little note with Tony's address and tossed it against the wall over my bed then returned to my homework. He could wait until he turned blue in the face. I wouldn't be going anywhere near his house. Not after his oh-so-welcoming invitation.

It was 3:20 P.M. when I was done with my algebra and rose from the desk to get a drink. The small Post-it ball had rolled in front of the door. With an annoyed grunt, I kicked it aside. But when I came back from the bathroom with a glass of water, the ball had all my attention once again. Caving in, I bent to pick it up.

A deep sigh escaped me. Based on what I'd seen today, Tony was a genius. Gifted. And I really wanted his notes. Actually, if I wanted to catch up with the class in time, I *needed* them. So maybe I could drive to his house, fetch the notes, and leave before he got a chance to open his freaking mouth and be nasty again.

It was either that or talk to Jerry, who couldn't draw a stick figure. *Sorry, Jeremy, I just can't risk messing this up because of unusable notes.* But the prospect of getting help from Anthony *Moron* Mitchell churned my gut. I raked my hands through my hair as I slumped back onto my desk chair. Could my first week in Grover Beach have been any more complicated?

Probably not.

By 3:50 P.M., I had come to a decision, dumped it, then made up my mind once again. I needed the notes, so I steeled my nerves for another encounter with Tony.

Then I realized I was facing a different problem. I had to ask Chloe for her car, because, for one, I had no idea where Tony's house was and needed a navigation system, and two, it could be miles away. I crossed the hallway to Chloe's room, but before I knocked on her door, I hesitated. She was going to say no, I knew it. Her annoying attitude had been a surprise to me, but there was one thing I definitely knew about my cousin. If she was pissed, she was pissed for weeks.

Maybe if I apologized...

I sucked in a breath through clenched teeth. *She* had been the idiot, not me. And the thought of backing down caused my toes to curl in my boots. But four *months* in her house? I had to overcome my irritation and just put on a smile. I could do it. "I can do it. I can do it..." I knocked on her door.

No reply.

Did she know it was me? I scratched my head then knocked again. "Chloe, can I come in?"

No reply.

I lowered my glance to the toes of my boots. "Look, I'm

ANNA KATMORE

sorry about Saturday night. Can we maybe...er...just forget about it?"

No reply. Yeah, that was to be expected after the first two dismissals. I turned the knob and opened the door. "Chloe?"

She wasn't in her room. I looked over my shoulder, stepped through the door, and glanced around. Everything looked the same as it had Saturday morning when I had arrived—still the perfect copy of a bedroom in a Barbie Dreamhouse. No clothes littered the light gray parquet, no homework was scattered on her desk. I was probably the only untidy person in this house.

The white wood furniture and purple angora wool carpet made me want to fetch a doll and start playing tea party in Wonderland, like we used to do when we were younger. Chloe had always wanted to be Alice. It had been fine with me. I had much preferred to be the Mad Hatter, anyway.

Apart from the bedding, which was now a soft purple satin and not Cinderella on flannel anymore, nothing had changed in this room. The wood-paneled mansard picked up the color of the parquet, and I ran my fingers along one furrow as I walked to the open window. Chloe's room faced the street, so I wiped the sheer curtains aside and leaned out, looking down. Her car was gone. Dang. Now I had a serious problem.

I'd better find Aunt Pamela and ask for her car before she decided to go grocery shopping or something.

Leaving the room as I had found it, I loped down the stairs and walked into the kitchen, where my aunt was chopping veggies and dropping them into a pot. Not going out any time soon. I relaxed and put on a nonchalant expression. "Hi, Pam."

She looked up from her cooking and wiped her hands on her apron. "Hey, Sammy. What's up?"

"Can I borrow your car for a bit? I need to get some study stuff from a classmate. Chloe's gone, so I can't borrow hers."

"Sure." She refastened her thick, honey-colored ponytail and walked with me into the hallway where she gave me the keys. "So, how was your first day? Do you like your teachers? Already made new friends?"

Oh, she meant apart from the Chloe Clan that traveled the corridors only in a pack? "Yeah, I met some really nice people. Guess what? They asked me to join their cheerleading team." I gave a wry laugh, but then I scrunched up my face, wondering if maybe it was a good idea after all.

"But that's great. You love dancing," Pam said.

"Yeah, we'll see. I'll check it out tomorrow. Thanks for the keys." I waved at her, then rushed out into the garage, climbed into the black Volvo, and drove off as soon as the wide, roll-up door was fully open.

I punched Tony's address into the GPS, then fisted the note again and shoved it into my pocket. It turned out that he lived on the opposite side of town, about two miles away from my aunt's house, in a picture-book neighborhood. I pulled up in front of his door. His house was painted white and had a low picket fence. A small yard ran from the front around the side, probably to a bigger garden in the back. It looked pretty much like any other house on the street, apart from the color and design of the doors and windows. Much smaller than my aunt and uncle's mansion, but lovely. I grunted. Way too nice for a

ANNA KATMORE

jerk like him.

The clock on the dashboard flashed 4:15. What if I was too early? I looked around but didn't see him anywhere. He must have already gotten home, and I was just looking for a reason not to get out. I sat in the car for a couple more minutes, staring out the side window. Were good grades in AVE really worth coming here and facing Mr. Bad Manners? Unfortunately, I had to answer that with a whiny yes.

Drawing in a few deep breaths, I forced my fingers to uncurl from the steering wheel and got out of the car. Three steps led to the front door. I rang the bell then waited for a silhouette to move behind the frosty glass. A shadow appeared and seconds later the door swung open. A tall woman with shoulder-length hair as fair as Tony's greeted me with a smile. "Hello."

"Um, hi. I'm Samantha Summers. Is Anthony home?" When I clasped my hands, I realized I was actually sweating. It made me gnash my teeth behind my closed lips. How could I let a stupid guy turn me into a ball of nerves?

Mrs. Mitchell nodded, then she shouted over her shoulder, "Tony! A friend of yours is here."

Friend? No.

"Black hair?" came the answer from somewhere inside.

Now his mother drew her brows into a puzzled expression as she looked back at me. "Yes." She shrugged, and it seemed like an apology.

It wasn't her fault that her son was an ass, so I let her off with a smile.

"Give her the stack of notes! It's on the chest!"

He didn't intend to come to the door? Fine with me. A relieved breath escaped me, and I felt the knot in my stomach ease.

Mrs. Mitchell, however, seemed to be appalled by her son's behavior and tried to explain in a confused but sympathetic voice, "He just came home from practice. He hasn't showered yet and probably doesn't want to come out all sweaty. Boys, you know." She grimaced, and I appreciated her attempt to give me an excuse though she had no idea what was going on.

The door stood wide open as she went back to the broad wooden chest to get the notes for me. I caught a brief glimpse of the inside of the house. A long hallway opened into several rooms at either side. I liked the floor tiles. They were creamy white with a blue tile here and there.

My gaze snapped back to the blond woman when she shouted once more. "There are two stacks, Tony! Which one?"

"The left! No wait, the right. Ah, damn..."

I sucked in a sharp breath when he suddenly appeared from a door at the far end of the hallway. He was wearing cleats and white shorts with two blue stripes on either side. And that was all. Nothing else. *Holy shit!* My eyes fastened on his bulging pecs and abs that glistened with sweat, while he wiped his face with his bright blue jersey.

His mom smiled at me when he reached us, then she left us alone. *No!* I wanted to shout after her, but she was gone and had no idea of my sinking heart.

The moment Tony stood in front of me I couldn't

remember how to make my tongue function or where my voice had gone. Strangely enough, the only thing I could concentrate on was his six-pack and nice belly button. Gosh, I was pathetic! I forced my eyes up to his face, if only for a second.

Tony cast me an irritated glance. Then he pulled the sweaty jersey over his head and shielded his annoyingly perfect body from my gaze. "Get that staring under control, Summers," he grunted.

Yeah, well, I was working on it.

He grabbed one of the stacks of papers from the top of the chest, put it in a wide folder, and held it out to me, not inviting me in. "These are the main projects. Detailed descriptions are clipped to each sketch."

I took the folder from him silently, forcing my thoughts to focus on what he'd said instead of on his body. His sweat-dripping hair stuck to his forehead and stood out in sweet angles on top. Along with his heated red cheeks, it made him look much younger and nicer than he actually was.

"I'm sure you'll figure out what to do," he snapped, folding his arms over his chest. "If not, you can ask my aunt for help."

"Yeah, thanks." It came out flat, my frustration at his rudeness coming through.

"Just try not to spill nail polish on my notes, okay?"

Excuse me? I pulled my brows into a huffy frown. "I don't do nail polish."

"Yeah, whatever." He grabbed the edge of the door and certainly would have closed it in my face in a second.

"Anthony, wait. Please." I didn't know what had driven me

to say that, but at the same time I squared my shoulders and inhaled a deep breath, which I hoped would give me an extra half-inch of height.

To my surprise, Tony stopped and arched one eyebrow.

Oh God, what to do now? I bit the inside of my cheek, then I mumbled, "Why are you so annoyed with me? Did I do something to offend you?" Yeah, very subtle, Sam. I wanted to slap myself—even if I did want to know the answer.

His other eyebrow came up, too.

Dammit, I was running into a dead end. But I had to say something, so I tried the next best thing that came to my mind. "Listen, I know you think I enjoyed how Chloe made fun of you the other night. But I didn't." I shrugged. "I can't help being her cousin, but I don't see why that's such a problem for you. Anyway, you got your revenge when you tore me to pieces in AVE today."

When he still said nothing, I made a hopeful face. "So...I'd say we're even?"

A slow, cold smile crept to his lips. "Right." Then he slammed the door in my face.

Ah...yes. That made a crappy day perfect.

Done with staring at his shadow disappearing behind the frosty glass, I dragged my feet from his front yard, planted my butt in the car, and floored it home.

"Goddamned idiot!" When I banged my fist on the steering wheel, I wasn't even sure if I was cursing Tony or me. I'd made a freaking fool of myself trying to be friendly. And he was such a moron. I gritted my teeth and pressed even harder on the gas pedal, muttering, *"Don't spill nail polish on them, Summers. Don't powder them up with makeup, Summers. Please don't put them in the wash."* Right, because that's what I usually did with borrowed notes. Asshole.

I slammed on the brakes in front of a pedestrian crossing to let two preschoolers and their grandma pass and screamed my frustration with Tony to the roof of the car. "I hate you!"

The kids gaped at me through the windshield as the old lady ushered them more quickly across the street. I blew a ragged breath through my nose before I drove on.

Back in my uncle's garage, I grabbed the notes from the passenger seat and walked inside. Dropping them on the desk in my room, I slumped on my bed and tried to kill myself and my misery by pressing the pillow to my face. I gave up after ten seconds, threw the pillow in a corner, and gazed at the ceiling.

Why, *oh why*, did I have to run into this horrible guy on my first night in town?

My gaze swept across the room until it landed on Tony's portfolio. It was a dark red folder with random drawings on it. Mostly fancywork and evil-eyed faces. The pencil strokes were accurate, even in those sketches that he'd obviously made without much attention. Absent doodling while listening to the teacher—this was something I did often to my folders.

I got up and wheeled the swivel chair to my desk, sat down, and opened the portfolio. There were five sketches inside, one in charcoal and four in pencil. Several sheets were clipped to each picture, with notes written all over the place. Though the beauty of his art left me breathless, it was Tony's handwriting that drew my attention right now. On a closer look, the order within the chaos of his jottings became clear. Though boyish enough, the artist shone right through in the fact that he wrote in cursive— in his classy capital letters and the zestful loops of his G's and J's. I traced them with my finger, then I dragged my hands over my face. I must have completely lost my mind. This was just handwriting, oh my God.

From my own portfolio, I took out a large piece of paper, read through Tony's instructions on the first project, and then began to outline a human body. The task was to dress the person in 1970s-style clothes.

I was halfway done with the flaring bell-bottoms when the weak light in my room really started to get on my nerves. The large window was little help when the sun was already creeping toward the west and my room faced the opposite direction. The dining room, on the other side, had bright light. I packed my stuff and carried everything downstairs, where Pam was just finalizing neat bowls of chocolate mousse, which we'd get for dessert, no doubt.

"Hey, Sammy," she said and placed the bowls in the fridge. "Did you get what you needed?"

I lifted the two folders of artwork. "Right here. Do you mind if I spread my stuff on the dining room table for a while? I can't draw with bad light, and these projects are really important. I'll be gone before dinner."

"Don't worry, sweetie. It's still over an hour until your uncle gets home."

I fanned out my drawing utensils on the wide, glass-top

ANNA KATMORE

table and got to work. The hippie without a defined face in my picture got dark platforms and a shirt with a floral design. I enjoyed this drawing, nailing the shadows of the clothing perfectly by rubbing my finger over certain parts, blurring the lines. Just for fun, I portrayed the woman with long braids hanging from both sides of her face and a slim band around her head.

"The sleeves have to be a bit wider toward the wrists," my aunt said as she leaned over me and studied my picture. "They looked like the flare in the pants, really."

"Aren't you too young to have been part of that freaky era?" I teased her, but I made the changes she suggested.

"I was too young to be a hippie but I had an aunt who came right out of that time. When I spent the night over at her place, she often showed me funny photo albums of her and her husband." Wrinkles of a smile built around her eyes. "I laughed so hard at their crazy looks that sometimes she feared I'd choke."

Sheesh, I knew how that sounded. When Pam got into one of her laughing fits, she was like a vacuum cleaner, and it was impossible not to laugh with her, just because of the sound of it. Aunt Pamela had always been my favorite relative, even though she was only related by marriage. Uncle Jack and my father looked a lot alike, but otherwise the brothers had little in common. While my father was warm and caring, it seemed like Jack was first and foremost interested in prestige and only secondly in family. The ever-busy attorney. He was a nice guy, all right, but after seventeen years of knowing him, he still wasn't even half as close to me as Pam had been since she'd given me a stuffed Roger Rabbit for Christmas when I was four years old.

Pam drew out the chair next to me and sat down, leaning her elbows on the table. She pointed at the hem of the right pant leg on my drawing. "You know, if you added a small pleat here and a larger one here, the pants would look a lot wider and more authentic."

I tried to do what she said, and heck, she was right. But that was no surprise. Pam was an artist herself, creating beautiful canvases in water color and oil paint. The hallway and parlor were wallpapered with her awesome abstract paintings of people, landscapes, and buildings. While my parents did everything to support my talent, Aunt Pamela really *understood* what drawing meant to me.

"Mind if I bring in my easel and paint with you for a bit? The chicken can bake without my help." She seemed happy when I nodded.

It was nice to have her around for the next forty minutes. Pam was a funny person, warm, and always up to giving amazing feedback. She also skimmed through Tony's pictures and was impressed by such a great talent. Her gaze fell on the one artsy letter that stood out at the bottom right of each drawing. She frowned. "And *T* is for..."

"Total jerk," I muttered before I knew what I was saying.

Pam burst out laughing, and I bit my bottom lip. Then I added, "Well, his name is Anthony Mitchell, so I guess T is for Tony."

"I see." Her laughter ebbed away. "Just where have I heard that name before?" Her forehead creased with a frown and she tilted her head. "Is he tall and blond with blue, blue eyes?"

And a killer mouth, designed to get on my nerves? "Yep, that's him."

"I think Chloe dated him a few times last summer. He's a very nice boy."

Now I turned around to face her fully. "Nice? Ha! That's not the side of him I've gotten to know."

Pam scratched her brow. "Really? For weeks, Chloe didn't speak of anyone else but this guy. She was so happy when he finally asked her out. Unfortunately, it didn't last very long. Chloe cried for days when it was over."

"Is that so?" How strange. This clashed with the story Susan and the girls had told me. If Chloe had dumped him, why would she cry? And what had made her dump him in the first place? Had he been rude when he'd slept with her? To me it seemed he was an asshole 24/7, so that could easily have been it.

I pushed the thought aside. After all, it wasn't my concern.

A few minutes later, Chloe walked into the kitchen with her father and they both stopped to stare at us for a moment. Pam and I were messing around a bit. We were laughing really hard about a misplaced brushstroke of hers that made the guy in her picture, who was apparently supposed to resemble Uncle Jack, look horny and ready for action.

"Hi, darling," Pam said as Jack came to kiss her on the cheek. "Sorry, we didn't hear you come in."

"I noticed that." He slung his arms around her hips and

studied the painting. "Is that me? And is *that* intentional?"

The three of us laughed again, but not Chloe. She stood rigid in the entrance to the dining room and scowled at me like I had eaten the last piece of her beloved white chocolate with strawberry filling.

"Hi, Chloe." I tried for a friendly voice, one with a conciliatory tone.

She just snorted, then ran her long fingers through her pigtails. "Mom, where's Rosa? I'm starving."

"I gave her the day off, honey," Pam answered. "It's her son's birthday and she wanted to spend it with him."

"Great. So am I supposed to have a soda for dinner?" Chloe muttered.

Pamela wiggled out of her husband's arms with a proud beam. "Dinner is almost ready. I cooked tonight."

"You?" both my uncle and Chloe blurted out.

I didn't know what was so special about that, but then I hadn't lived in this house long enough to know all the house rules.

"Yes. Me." Somewhat irritated, Pam walked to the stove. "I cooked before Rosa came to us, and none of you ever complained."

Jack laid his arm around his daughter's shoulders. He looked at my aunt with a mild expression. "There was no need for you to get your hands dirty, Pam. We can go out for dinner anytime."

Pamela pulled delicious-smelling chicken parmesan out of the oven and placed the tray on the marble counter. "It's no big deal. In fact, I've always enjoyed cooking. I was really looking forward to doing it today." Her shoulders slumped a little. "Please, don't spoil it for me now. Let's just eat." Her warm smile reappeared as she looked at me. "Can I get you to clear the table, Sammy?"

With that stupid drama going on, my butt had frozen to the chair, the pencil still clenched between my fingers. I jumped up from my seat. "Of course."

We didn't have a Rosa back in Cairo, or anywhere we had lived in the past. My mom always cooked for us. I'd thought it totally normal to find Pam in the kitchen today. Obviously, in this house it was not.

I packed up Tony's and my sketches and rushed upstairs. After I washed my hands, I came back down to a nicely decorated dining room table. I slid into the seat opposite my cousin and held out my plate as Pam dished out the chicken.

Everyone was silent. I wondered if Pam's cooking was a bigger issue than I had thought. At least they seemed to like the food, because Jack and Chloe both tucked in like there was no tomorrow.

"That," I said around a bite, pointing my fork to the second helping of chicken on my plate, "tastes fabulous, Pam."

She looked at me from the corner of her eye and her lips curved in a happy smile. "Thank you, honey."

Chloe's head snapped up so fast that I almost dropped my fork. She scowled at me, then at her mom, and finally at me again. Sometimes that girl totally weirded me out. All the more reason to make up with her, and make up fast.

"Hey, Chloe," I said and took a sip from my lemonade. "I thought we could hang out a bit tonight, maybe grab some ice cream and watch a DVD or something."

"Actually, I'm meeting up with Brin and Kir in an hour. We're going to see a movie in town." Cold, emotionless. I hated the aversion she shoved in my direction.

"You should take Sam with you," Pamela suggested, and Jack agreed with a nod.

I wondered if her father's approving look was the reason Chloe finally blew a strand of unnaturally blond hair out of her eyes and said, "Fine. Be ready at eight."

Okay, not the warm invitation I had hoped for, but it was better than nothing. Maybe we could start over again.

After dinner, I changed my clothes, ran a comb through my unruly hair, and brushed my teeth. I was outside waiting by Chloe's car at three minutes to eight. She gave an irritated snort when she saw me standing there.

We both climbed in, then she started the engine and cruised down the road. This was the perfect moment to talk things out with her.

"Listen, Clo, I wanted to tell you sorry for what happened down in the café. I was a little stressed out and—"

The tires screeched to a halt. I was pressed into the seatbelt so hard that all the air whizzed out of my lungs. "What the heck—" I gasped.

Chloe turned a cold look on me. "Get out."

"What?"

"Get out of my car."

"Why?"

"Because if you don't, I'll just come around and drag you out by your hair."

Oh my God! What had gotten into the girl? "Chloe, if this is because of Saturday night, let me—"

"Samantha, I have no intention of bringing you with me to meet my friends. Never did. I said yes so my mom and dad would get off my back, but now I want you to get out and find something else to do."

Wow. I swallowed hard. Her face was etched in granite, so I figured arguing further was useless. I unbuckled my seatbelt and opened the door, but before I could get out, I heard her cold voice behind me.

"And stay away from Pamela Summers. She's not your mother, she's mine. *Yours* is miles away and obviously not very interested in you, or she wouldn't have sent you to my place to squeeze in where you don't belong."

My chest tightened at her words. Not because I believed the shit she said, but because I couldn't understand so much hatred coming from a girl I'd loved to hang out with all my life. I was too wrung up to reply, so I climbed out and slammed the door shut behind me, heading down the sidewalk and not turning around when the tires screeched away from the curb.

CHAPTER 5

ALL RIGHT, WHAT to do with an evening that went wrong before it had even started? I dropped my suddenly exhausted self onto a bench close to the road and fished in my pocket for my cell phone. I had called my parents several times since coming to my aunt's place, and I always made sure to sound happy and not convey how much I missed them. But when I called my mom tonight, I just sobbed into the phone.

I told her about Chloe's unexpected bitchiness and that she was turning my stay into hell. I also told her about Anthony Mitchell's verbal slaps in the face. My mom listened to my rant for minutes without disrupting me, then she took a deep breath before she turned into the angel I knew. She asked me about the good moments I'd already had in Grover Beach. I remembered Susan, Lisa, and Simone, who seemed to instantly like me, and I also told her that Nick Frederickson had done the fish dissecting for me when I couldn't.

As usual, my mom's soft voice soothed me. By the time I said good night and promised that I would call her after school tomorrow, I'd dabbed at my tears and was able to breathe again without my chest and throat feeling like they were being acupunctured.

I sat for a little while, regarding the darkening sky, wondering whether I should just go home and go to bed. Yeah, great idea, coming home with eyes bloodshot from crying. My aunt and uncle would freak out. And Chloe would have my head for it. I planted my boots on the bench and hugged my knees to my chest, skimming through the new names in my cell phone. Maybe one of the girls was up to having a cappuccino with me in Charlie's café.

My thumb hovered over the call button with Lisa's name on the display. She was probably with her boyfriend, and I didn't want to be the odd one out. I called Susan instead.

"Hi, Sam, what's up?" she greeted me with a happy giggle. "We were just talking about you."

"Um...hi. Who is *we*, and why were you talking about me?"

"I'm with Lisa, Simone, and then some. Wanna come hang out with us?"

I hesitated, deliberating who *some* would be. But she could mean anybody, and I desperately needed a little distraction right now. "Sure. Where are you guys?"

"At Hunter's beach house. Where are you? I can come and get you."

Chloe hadn't gone far before she'd kicked me out, so I figured it was best to walk back home and have Susan pick me up from there. "Do you know where Chloe lives?"

A snort traveled down the line. "Yes."

I laughed at her obvious disgust. "Know what? I'll wait for you at the corner down the street. How's that?"

"Much better than picking you up right from her driveway.

T is for...   67

I'll be there in ten."

I rang off and walked toward the point where we were supposed to meet. Susan and I arrived there at the same time. She was fast.

The window rolled down on the passenger's side. A beaming Susan leaned over. "Get your pretty ass in."

I did, and she drove off in silence. After a couple of minutes, she asked, "What's with your eyes?"

"Long story." And nothing I really wanted to talk about.

But obviously Susan did. "Trouble in the house of Summers?"

Gazing out the side window, I sighed. "Sort of."

"Chloe gave you shit again, didn't she?"

Now I turned to her. "Again?" What did this girl know?

"Right before you called me, Lisa told us what happened Saturday night down at Charlie's."

A grunting sound traveled up my throat. "Let's just say it's not as much fun to live with her as I'd hoped."

Susan glanced at me, then back out the windshield. She was silent, but I knew she was dying to hear the full story—all the gory details.

All right. "I tried to make up with Chloe, and she said I could come with her and her friends to see a movie. But it was just a show for her parents. In fact, later, she kicked me out, making it clear in no uncertain terms that she wanted me gone, not only from her car, but also from her house and her family."

"Ouch."

"Yeah...ouch." And Susan didn't even know half of how

68   ANNA KATMORE

much this really hurt.

"Ah, forget about that bimbo. You can hang out with us any time you want. Just give me a call and I'll spring you from the Summers' dungeon."

Her humor cheered me up, and by the time we arrived at Ryan's place, which was a nice bungalow down on the beach just outside town, a smile curved my lips again. Susan steered her car into an empty spot that looked like it was waiting just for her, then we climbed out. A weird feeling settled in my gut as she led me up to the wraparound porch and knocked on the door. Laughter drifted from inside. And familiar voices. *Damn.* My heart lurched to my throat. Tony was with them. I didn't know how much more of *him* I could bear tonight.

Lisa opened the door a few seconds later, smiling at me. She ushered me in after Susan when I was hesitant. "What are you waiting for, Sam? Come on in."

After a deep breath, I followed her through a spacious living room and into the kitchen. A bunch of people sat squeezed around a rectangular wooden table. Some of them I knew, others I didn't. They all turned our way when we came in and shouted greetings or waved at me.

Tony was rocking on two legs of his chair, his eyes narrowed to a scowl. Of course he didn't say anything.

I forced my gaze away from him and said, "Hi, all," to everyone else.

Lisa pointed a chair out to me, across from her and between Nick Frederickson and a dark-haired woman I hadn't seen before. "This is Rachel and her husband, Phil," Lisa introduced us. "Rachel's Ryan's sister."

I shook hands with her, noticing the stunning likeness of the siblings.

They were all sharing pizza from five huge boxes. Ryan offered me a piece on a paper plate the moment I sat down. In spite of my smile, I still felt utterly miserable inside, and pizza was the last thing I wanted. But I figured it would be rude to refuse. I really wanted to blend in, so I forced a few bites down but declined a second piece.

"Chloe is being a glorious bitch again."

I nearly choked as a sip of Sprite went down the wrong pipe at Susan's announcement.

Lisa looked at me as if she totally knew what horror I'd been through. "What did she do this time?"

I could do nothing but shake my head as I coughed, fighting to get air into my lungs again. Susan didn't shut up. She babbled out all the information she'd wrung from me on the drive here. The boys rolled their eyes, and the girls scrunched their faces in sympathy.

"That's so ugly of her," said Simone and smacked Alex on the shoulder. "I can't believe you made out with her last year, too. Does no man ever see what a bitch she is?"

Alex rubbed the spot on his shoulder where he got hit and grinned. "Hey, don't give me that. I didn't know her back then. And seriously, you don't care about things like *bitch or not* if you're a guy." He smirked at Nick, who burst out laughing, then he leaned in and kissed Simone on the mouth. "But now I'm with you, so no need to worry, baby." He took a big bite from

ANNA KATMORE

the slice of pizza she held in her hand, which was obviously the end of their argument.

The conversation soon focused on soccer. I pulled a lollipop from my pocket, unwrapped it, popped it in my mouth, and leaned back in the chair, just listening. Until I noticed Lisa watching me. One eyebrow raised in inquiry, I waited for her to tell me what was on her mind. She leaned on the table and lowered her voice so as not to interrupt her boyfriend and Nick. They were having a discussion about the best tactics to score a goal on a team from L.A. that apparently called themselves the Rabid Wolves.

"I'm having a sleepover at my place on Friday," said Lisa. "Just us girls. Allie will be there, too. Wanna come?"

That sounded like a nice idea. I yanked the lollipop out of my mouth. "Sure. Where's your place?"

Lisa tore off a piece of pizza box and scribbled her address on it. Apart from one number, the address was totally identical to Tony's. Of course, she'd told me they were best friends, but I didn't realize they lived next to each other.

"You two are neighbors?" I said, looking from her to Tony and back, which gave me everybody's immediate attention. *Well done, Sam.*

"Yeah, always have been," Lisa said with a light quirk of her brows. "So you know where Tony lives?"

I wasn't prepared for the innuendo in her question. In fact, it was totally out of place. An annoying warmth crept to my cheeks.

"Oh, come on, don't be ridiculous," Tony said before I

could answer. His laughter sounded irritated. "My aunt forced me to give her my AVE notes, and she came to get them this afternoon. I'm not hanging out with another *Summers*. You should know me better than that."

Even though I was prepared for shit coming from *him*, the way he emphasized my name stabbed me in the chest.

"By the way, *tiny*." He turned his pissed glare at me. "Shouldn't you be home drawing?"

Yeah, right. Maybe he wanted to show me to the door, too? Could it be that he and Chloe shared the same gene pool? Their manners sucked, and I was so at my limit tonight. So I snapped back, "And shouldn't you be in a café wiping tables, *busboy*?"

The others sucked in a collective breath. Apparently I'd hit a nerve, and I regretted my words the instant they left me. Tony's glare turned from stone cold to freezing. His mouth curved in the parody of a grin. "Only on weekends, hun."

The term of endearment had the effect of a combine harvester running down my spine. Our gazes locked in a scowling battle as he continued, "So if you intend to show up with your sweet cousin, let me know and I'll hold a table for you. In the basement. Where we keep the other snakes."

My chin dropped to my chest and my throat tightened painfully. I'd run out of comebacks to his low blows.

Lisa punched his arm. "Hey, don't give her crap. She's already getting enough of it from her cousin."

"Why? She started it."

"How?" I suddenly screamed at him. "By coming in this house? By moving to this town? Or simply by being born a

72   ANNA KATMORE

Summers?" My vision misted. I quickly blinked the welling tears away and rose from the chair. Clearing my throat, I turned a pleading look to Lisa. "Could you show me to the bathroom, please?"

"Sure." She stood and smacked Tony upside his head. "Sometimes you're such an idiot."

I followed her out of the kitchen to the back of the house, where she pointed out the bathroom. "You okay?" she said, rubbing my arm.

"Yeah. I just need a minute."

"Look, normally Tony isn't such an ass. His poor male brain is just taking a while to understand that not every person named Summers is like Chloe."

I nodded but didn't want to discuss it right now when new tears were crowding my eyes. Lisa squeezed my hand, which was comforting, then headed back to the front and I locked myself in the bathroom. I sat on the edge of the peach-colored tub for a couple of minutes, blowing my nose on toilet paper. Eventually, I went to the double sink and splashed cold water on my face.

With my hands braced on the soft-pink marble counter, I looked at myself in the mirror. Oh, what a fine appearance I made. Shoving my hair out of my eyes, I took a few deep breaths. Just why did this bastard get under my skin so much? He was a jackass. Someone not even worth a second thought. But it was impossible to brush off his jibes. The truth was they hurt more than I wanted to admit. I didn't want to face him again.

However, staying in here for the rest of the night was not

an option. My stomach knotted as I turned the lock. I slipped out and silently closed the bathroom door just as a harsh whisper drifted to me from a room at the other end of the hall.

"What the hell was that in there?"

I recognized Lisa's voice and stopped dead.

"What do you mean?" That was Tony, sounding arrogant as usual.

Instinctively, I stepped back and pressed myself against the bathroom door. This could only be about me. And I wasn't sure if I wanted to eavesdrop. But what other choice did I have? If I walked back to the kitchen now, they'd see me and know I heard them. I wanted that even less than hearing what they had to say.

"I mean you and Sam. I wasn't sure if you two were going to make out on the kitchen table or tear out each other's throats."

Oh boy, had she completely lost it?

Obviously, Tony thought the same. "Are you out of your mind, Liz?" He stressed each word.

"Tony, I'm certainly the person who's known you best for most of your life. But ever since Sam entered the café on Saturday, it seems like I don't know you at all. Why are you such a dickhead when she's around?"

"Because..."

"Because what?" Lisa demanded when he fell silent.

I, too, tensed for his answer. But Tony decided to counter with his own question. "Why would you think I'd want to make out with her? Have you looked at her? She's totally not my type."

ANNA KATMORE

Okay, I knew that, but still...*ouch.*

"She's a pretty girl."

"She's not. She's short. And snappy. Did you hear how she called me *busboy*? That is totally Chloe's word. And what's with her hair? Does she comb it with a firecracker or what? Someone should tell her she looks like a hobbit."

"Anthony Jason Mitchell, that's a friend of mine you're talking about! Why are you suddenly turning into a complete moron? Someone should spank some sense into you."

"Knock it off, Liz," he said, annoyed. "You sound like my mother."

"If Eileen Mitchell could hear you now, she'd ground you for the rest of the century," Lisa whispered harshly. Then she continued, sounding a little calmer, "By the way, I like Sam's hair. It's cool and something new. I'm thinking about getting a similar style myself, actually."

Tony chuckled. "Yeah, do that and Hunter will spank *your* ass. And if he doesn't, I will."

A moment later, he came out of the room and walked straight for the kitchen. He didn't see me pressed against the bathroom door, horrified by what he'd just said.

Lisa, however, spotted me the instant she came out after him. With a grimace, she stopped in her tracks. "Oh no. You heard it all, didn't you?"

I nodded, unable to speak.

"I'm so sorry. I shouldn't have cornered him in there."

Now I shook my head, wanting her to stop apologizing. It certainly wasn't her fault Tony was an asshole. In fact, I was the idiot for listening in on them. "Could you give me a ride home?" I begged. "I don't want to go in there again."

Lisa waited a moment, as if deliberating whether to attempt to persuade me to stay. Finally, she nodded in resignation. "Sure. Just let me get Ryan's keys."

"I'll wait outside."

With a spinning mind, I trudged through the front room and out onto the veranda, where I slumped down on the wooden steps. Only twenty feet away, waves crashed on the beach, and I wished I could drown all my anger and pain in them. I was so sick of this whole moving thing and the troubles that came with it.

Sniffing, I wiped my nose with the back of my hand. When the door opened behind me two minutes later, I glanced over my shoulder. It wasn't Lisa coming out but her boyfriend. He jingled a bunch of keys in his hand. My butt remained rooted to the floorboards as he walked down the steps, turned around, and squatted in front of me.

"Tough day, huh?" he said, looking me in the eye.

"You have no idea."

"I told Lisa I'd take you home. You cool with that?"

"Um, sure." As long as I would get away from Tony, all was fine with me.

"Okay, let's go." He rose and reached for my hand, pulling me up.

In a car that certainly commanded attention wherever it was, Ryan drove me home. Most of the way we were silent, but when he turned into the street where my family lived, he slowed down and looked at me for the first time. "You know, he isn't really such a jerk."

"Who, Tony?" *Yeah, right.* "That's a bit hard to believe," I muttered.

"Seriously. He's a nice guy. A good friend. I've known him for a long time." He parked the car in front of the house and cut off the engine, which made me wonder if he had more to say.

I unbuckled my seatbelt and turned toward him. "Why are you telling me this?"

"Because my girl likes you, and from what I'm getting, you're cool. Seems like you'll be hanging out with us a lot in the future. I just want you to feel comfortable when you do."

"Comfortable?" I gave a bitter laugh. "With Anthony Mitchell around? Oh, sure."

"Give him a chance. He just needs some time to...adjust. He'll work it out, I'll make sure of it." When Ryan started the engine again, he smirked at me. "Mitchell is a soccer player. It's all about defense. He doesn't like it when somebody's getting under his skin."

My brows pulled into a nonplussed frown.

"Never mind." Ryan laughed. "Go to bed and get some rest. I think you need it—you look chewed up and spat out. See you at school. Lisa will save a seat for you at lunch."

I didn't know if I should be happy about that or scared. Hanging out with Lisa and her friends was nice. Hanging out with Tony was...like a tonsillectomy without anesthesia. "Thanks for the ride," I told him and heaved a sigh.

Ryan said good night, then I climbed out of his car. As he

drove off, I headed inside, grateful that I had my own keys this time. All the crap I'd had to take tonight had exhausted me, and I fell asleep within minutes.

*

Before school the next day, I ran Tony's notes through the copier in my uncle's office. I would give them back to him at lunchtime and then find a seat with Allie and her friends. I had strained Tony's generosity enough by borrowing his notes. From now on I would give him a wide berth. After I got my school bag from my room, I left the house a bit early, so there was no need to run this morning.

Science was fun, with Nick crying because we had to dissect an onion, and I was looking forward to the classes in which I would sit next to Susan again. She'd asked me to sit over with her in science, too, but Nick wouldn't let me go.

Lisa, Susan, Simone, and I ran late at lunch because we'd gotten distracted by a poster hanging in the corridor that announced an upcoming soccer game. Apparently, the day was the date of Lisa and Ryan's three-month anniversary. Lisa didn't like the fact that Ryan hadn't told her he'd be busy.

Ten minutes later, we entered the cafeteria ranting about how boys never appreciated the important things in a relationship. Most of the tables were full and the buffet nearly empty. With a queasy feeling in my stomach, I cut a glance at the long table where Nick and the guys sat, but Tony wasn't with them. Scanning the entire room, I couldn't make him out anywhere else either. Shit. I really wanted the notes out of my backpack and the last time I'd speak to him done. But it seemed I'd have to carry them with me a bit longer. At least I could sit with my friends without the tension of his presence.

I lowered into the same chair as yesterday, right beside Nick. Leaning across the table, I asked Lisa if Tony wasn't here because of me. She shifted in her seat and mumbled, "Of course not." But she didn't sound at all convincing. I guessed they might have had another argument over me last night, which totally freaked me out. But I didn't say anything more and just tried to enjoy my small heap of spaghetti.

The meal was a mistake, though, because it kept traveling back up my gullet when we had to do cartwheels and some jumping on a giant trampoline in PE. Or maybe that was just due to the disgust that rose inside me when I thought of facing Tony in my next class.

Before the bell rang for the last period, AVE, I took a deep breath, straightened to my full five-two, and stalked up to Tony at the back of the room. He didn't notice me. Good, I thought, and dropped his folder in front of him on the desk, not caring that he was just jotting something down on a sheet of paper and the portfolio landed on his hand. "Thank you," I said in the most emotionless tone I could manage.

Baffled for the length of a breath, Tony looked up and quirked his brows. "You're done with all the projects?"

Oh. So that's what he sounded like when he didn't behave like a pig. Nice. But I knew I'd startled him, and that was the only reason he'd spoken to me in the first place. By now he probably regretted opening his mouth. Anyway, I didn't want to waste another couple of seconds of my precious time on him.

"I'm done with the first," I told him in a noncommittal voice. "I photocopied your stuff this morning so I could get it off my desk and not run the risk of spilling *nail polish* all over it." Then I flashed a cold smirk at him, turned on the spot, and walked to the front before he could come up with a shitty reply. Sliding into my seat, I exhaled a satisfied breath.

Mrs. Jackson walked in and started the lesson just two minutes later. Soon, the strange sensation of someone's gaze lingering on the back of my neck had me raking an uncomfortable hand through my hair. I tried to concentrate on our teacher, but the feeling was hard to ignore. After twenty minutes, I dared a brief look over my shoulder, expecting to see Tony's eyes boring into me with a death glare. But they weren't. He was focusing on the front of the classroom. Except, after his next blink, he cut a glance at me and we locked gazes. Weird. I couldn't look away. And he didn't look his normal, pissed-off self. Just...expressionless.

I gritted my teeth and turned around. *Anthony Mitchell, I'm done with you.*

Class was over fast, but not a lot had registered. When the bell rang, I had to ask Laura Evans, the girl sitting next to me, about the homework. She let me quickly copy her notes, then I stuffed my things into my backpack and headed out after a small group of students.

Outside the building, I ran into Allie. "Hey, Sam," she said. "We're going to meet up for training on the soccer field in a few minutes. You coming?"

Some dancing was just what I needed after getting a stiff neck in class. And since I had decided to give the cheerleader thing a shot after all, I nodded and followed her to the trimmed lawn a few hundred meters from the school. We were the first to arrive. I slumped down under a tree while we waited for the others. By and by, they joined us, and in the end we were a total of eight girls.

Lisa sat down Indian-style next to me and bumped her shoulder against mine. "How was art? Did the oaf behave?"

"Yeah, everything was cool." I shrugged. "No insults for once."

"Good. I told him I'd kick his ass from here to Nebraska if he was mean to you ever again."

So I was right about them having another argument last night. It hadn't been necessary, because I'd be out of his path from now on anyway, but it was nice to hear that Lisa was standing up for me. I bumped her shoulder back. "Thanks."

A moment later, Allie had us stretching our muscles before we started the training. With the sole of my right foot planted against a tree trunk, I did some stretches like I used to do in ballet class as a child. I reached for my toes and touched my forehead to my shin then turned my head to the side and let my gaze roll out onto the soccer field. Some boys and girls were running out on the grass. So it was co-ed training today. I tried to find Susan in the crowd. She must have been there somewhere, but I couldn't spot her. Instead, I caught a glimpse of Anthony Mitchell.

He wore the white shorts and blue jersey again, and now I saw that there was an evilly grinning red shark on everyone's back. The same as on the banner hanging from the bleachers that spelled *Grover Beach Bay Sharks*.

Tony swung around, his gaze landing on our small group. Too late, I realized that I'd been watching him pass the ball with Nick. He sure noticed, because his eyes narrowed when our gazes met for a second before he turned away and jogged off toward the goal.

TONY

AS I RAN out onto the field with Hunter and the others, I was still gnashing my teeth. I couldn't believe my lack of attention when the gnome had dumped my stuff on my desk and actually rendered me speechless for a second.

Nick aimed a kick at me. "Do some passing for warm-up?"

We kicked back and forth for a minute, running along the side of the field, trying hard not to get into Chloe's line. Well, I did. I had enough crazy going on since last night and didn't care for bumping into her, too.

At the far end of the field, Nick and I switched positions, and there I spotted the girls. Allie had made it a point that we all train at the same time, so we could give them feedback afterward. Nothing I was really eager about. Girls dancing was, well...if you were a guy you would like it, whether they were pros or not.

Normally, I enjoyed them for a few minutes but then concentrated on the game and afterward told them they were cool. But this time I knew Lisa would be with them. My blood pressure rose in anticipation of seeing her cheering for us.

I had been dumbstruck when she'd announced it yesterday during lunch. But then she'd joined the soccer team for me last summer, so why not be a cheerleader for Hunter now? I searched the small group for her beautiful, long hair. What I got stuck on, though, was a thatch of black weed attached to a body that could stretch like a fucking bungee cord.

The little gnome had her leg bumped up on a tree and was bending forward like she was made of fucking rubber. She quickly looked away. Yeah right, like I hadn't noticed her staring at me.

Seriously, with all the shit I'd given her last night, it surprised me that she could still look at me and not throw up. Damn, Samantha Summers was probably a nice girl. She must be if Liz had befriended her the very first day. And logically, I knew she and Chloe Summers weren't the same person. Still...better keep a distance. I'd had my fair share of trouble with one of them and I didn't need another story I couldn't tell to anybody afterward.

I raced Nick with headers to the upper end of the field, then we kicked back and forth once more. At the end of it, I sneaked another glance at the girls, who were now practicing some easy steps to music. Lisa laughed when they were all supposed to roll their hips, and I couldn't look away until she'd done it.

Fuck, just why had I let that girl go? She twisted her hair up and fixed it with a claw at the back of her head. Nothing the bungee gnome could ever do with *her* hair. She just shoved it out of her face and tried to hook it behind her ears, which didn't work out. Short as it was, it immediately slid to the front again. She blew the bangs out of her eyes, then unzipped her hoodie and tossed it to the side.

Holy shit!

Sam wore little to nothing underneath. Just a black top that ended right below her ribs and pressed her boobs to her body. It was laced in the back, and together with the camo pants and the heavy black boots she seemed to wear permanently, the bungee gnome suddenly looked a damn lot like Lara Croft. I stopped with the ball under my foot and blatantly watched while she showed the others some street dance moves. With the little she wore on top, this was the sexiest thing I'd ever seen.

Pain exploded in my head as a ball hit me right above my left ear. Cussing and with a roaring head, I stumbled to the side.

"Stop staring at my girl, Mitchell!" Hunter shouted as he came running to me, laughing. He knew I wouldn't touch Lisa as long as she was with him. He also knew this would change the very instant one of them decided to break up. However, this time his bantering was far off.

"I wasn't staring at your—" *Yeah right. Tell him who you were really looking at.* I almost laughed at myself. "Ah, forget it. Let's play." I grabbed the soccer ball he'd tossed at me and ran up to the opposite goal to get voted into either Hunter's or Winter's team. As always, I ended up Hunter's first pick.

CHAPTER 6

THE CHEERLEADING WAS fun. Nothing like I had expected, really. When Allie asked me to show them more intricate moves and they all found them pretty cool, I thought it wouldn't hurt to stick with the girls. In the end it was clear that we weren't the usual kind of cheerleaders, jumping and shouting and doing the splits. Instead, we aimed for a mix of hip-hop and funk. Even the few weeks of Zumba classes I'd taken a couple of years ago came in handy with salsa steps and body rolls. I liked what we did, and the rest of them apparently did, too.

We went for some ice cream after training, but I excused myself early, because I had to work on my drawing. With the homework we'd gotten in AVE, which was sketching a female fantasy villain, I wanted to make good on the time I'd missed. I decided to go for a harpy with leathery wings, a raven's beak and a rat's tail with a spear at the end. After I finished this one, I only managed to get half of another project done, then I did my math homework and wrote a funky poem about my boots for English literature. During all that work, I also got to know Rosa, the cook.

Later, I sat through a queasy dinner with Chloe and her parents that featured a really weird conversation.

ANNA KATMORE

"It was your first cheerleading practice today, wasn't it, Sammy?" Pamela asked me midway through dinner.

I looked up from my meal and answered with a nod.

"Did you like it?"

"It was okay. I'm actually thinking of continuing to do it. I guess it's better to dance with them than not at all."

Pam beamed at me across the table. "I'm sure you made the right decision."

"Cheerleading, ha!" With a high-pitched laugh, Chloe poked her father in the side with her elbow. "The good ones play the real sport, don't they, Dad?"

He nodded and dabbed at his mouth with an embroidered napkin. "How's your penalty kick doing? Have you improved since last summer?"

Chloe smirked. "I scored seven goals out of ten last week. Hunter says I'm one of his best players."

Yeah, that's probably the only reason he kept her on a team where no one really liked her. I snorted, but quickly shoved a slice of carrot into my mouth to smother the sound.

Pamela ignored her husband and daughter's chat and looked at me with gleaming eyes. "I still have my cheerleading uniform from my own high school days. If you want, you can try it on later. I can alter it for you if it's too long."

Wow, that was a generous offer. "Thanks, but we're not dancing in uniform. It's just a fun thing, and Allie—she's sort of the captain—lets us wear whatever we want. She even finds it cool that I wear my camo pants and boots, because it fits the dance style we're practicing right now."

T is for...

Chloe turned cold eyes on me. "You seriously call that stomping and those stupid spasms you do a *style*?" She jerked her body from side to side to ridicule our moves.

"Chloe!" Pam hissed in a sharp voice I hadn't heard since my cousin and I both fell into their swimming pool behind the house when we were seven years old and fully dressed. "I'm sure the girls know what they're doing. And since you're not part of it, you're not going to badmouth their dancing. I won't have that in our house. Do I make myself clear?"

As if Pam's defending me wasn't bad enough, she also placed a hand on top of mine in support. Chloe's disgusted stare felt like she was pinching my skin with little pricks. Finally, her eyes snapped up to mine. Beneath all the ice in her gaze, I thought I spotted a tiny flicker of pain. She ran a napkin over her lips, then tossed it onto her half-finished meal and stood. "May I be excused, Dad? I still have homework to do."

"Of course, darling," he told her.

We all watched as she stalked out the door. I was happy when I'd finished my dinner and could head to my room as well. I didn't understand why Chloe was so jealous every time Pamela and I seemed to have something in common, something we could talk about or do together. It wasn't like I was trying to steal her mom to replace my own. Dammit, I missed my parents. Nothing and no one could replace them for me. So what was wrong with trying to adapt to the given situation and be a nice guest instead of an annoying burden?

I called my mother, because I had forgotten to do it after school, and told her only about the good things that had

ANNA KATMORE

happened since our last call. She didn't need to hear about the hobbit insult last night or Chloe's jealousy freak shows. It felt good to hear Mom's voice. She told me how much she and Dad missed me before we rang off. After the call, I studied a little history for the test tomorrow. Most of the stuff I already knew by heart, so I didn't worry about failing at all.

Wednesday, for once, went by peacefully and gave me hope for a quiet rest of the week. I wasn't disappointed. Tony was there at lunch breaks, but he always kept the greatest possible space between us. Thus, I considered it safe to sit with my friends. Occasionally, I caught his cold gaze on me in AVE, but when Mrs. Jackson picked my sketches to discuss with the rest of the class again, he didn't say a word. I wondered if it was Lisa's threats that kept him silent. If so, I was really grateful.

On Friday, I went to school in a lighter frame of mind, filled with anticipation for Lisa's sleepover. Someone had mentioned *Warm Bodies* and "tons of chocolate ice cream". Though never a real fan of zombie movies, I totally loved Nicholas Hoult and didn't care if he ate brains for a while as long as he got to kiss the girl in the end.

Unfortunately, Alyssa Silverman squashed my dream of Nicholas and ice cream during lunch break. She came over and pulled out a chair next to Lisa. "Sorry, guys." Her gaze skated over us. "I can't come to the sleepover tonight. Is there any chance we can delay this until tomorrow?" First she looked sheepish, but then a wide grin stretched her lips.

"What came up?" Lisa asked.

Funny thing, it was Sasha who answered that question. Not

looking at any of us, he carefully lifted his slice of pizza to his mouth without dripping any of the molten hot cheese and said, "I asked her out. She said yes." He bit off the corner and cracked a smile.

None of us said anything, although we were all dying to hear how that went. We would have to wait until the break was over and we could corner her during gym for details...which we were *so* going to do.

I saw Lisa squeeze Allie's hand in shared glee, then she cast the rest of us a questioning look. "Who's okay with coming over on Saturday?"

And gone was a good Friday night.

"Sure, count me in," said Susan. Since Simone was chewing on a big bite of burger, she only lifted her hand.

I shrugged one shoulder. "'K, that's cool."

The prospect of hanging out at my aunt's house tonight with a melodramatic Chloe around made me reach into my pocket for a cherry lollipop to sweeten up my mood.

Hunter slipped his hand under Lisa's hair and pouted. "That means I won't get to see you at all this weekend."

I knew why he was depressed, even though most of it was feigned. Some of the boys had planned a night out in the woods for when we girls would be by ourselves at Lisa's place. Now they would be out tonight and not allowed to join us tomorrow.

"You're a big boy. You'll survive," Lisa replied playfully.

"Or..." he drawled, letting his pout slip into a grin, "you girls could come camping with us."

Simone dropped her burger. "To the woods?" Yeah, she

didn't seem like she'd enjoy a night out in nature. But the look on Alex's face made me believe he'd just had a vision of how he'd make the time enjoyable for her.

"Sure, that's a great idea, baby," he told her. "We can sleep in the same tent and cuddle up in one sleeping bag. I'll even roast you marshmallows on the fire."

That was the moment when Simone's exasperation turned into a beam. "Let's do it!" It probably wasn't the marshmallow that had swayed her so fast.

Lisa, on the other hand, seemed a little skeptical. She glanced at Susan. "What do you think?"

"If you go, I'll go."

And then everyone looked at me.

A sudden swoosh of discomfort came over me. I sucked a little harder on my lollipop, then pulled it out with a smack. Apart from Ryan and Alex, I knew Nick and Tony would be there, too. Nick I could stomach, Tony...probably not. The grumpy look he was giving me made my gut roll with unease. "I don't know. I'm not that big a fan of camping. You know, without bathrooms, warm water, or cable."

Nick laughed and casually wrapped an arm around my shoulders. "Come on, Finn Girl. It'll be fun."

"Yeah, and I need someone to sleep in a tent with me, anyway," Susan pointed out. "I'm not gonna sleep alone with all the coyotes and bears out there. And you can't team me up with one of those jerks." She nodded her head toward Tony and Nick, but we all knew she liked them both big time, so no one took offense.

I made a wry face. "There aren't any bears left in California, you know."

"Doesn't matter. I want you to come."

"Me, too," said Lisa and gave me a pleading look.

"Yeah, me, too," Simone agreed.

And then Alex, Nick, and Ryan all repeated what the girls had said. I was really flattered, looking from one to the next, my smile spreading wider. I didn't expect Tony to comment on it, but the others were apparently awaiting his approval nonetheless. When they all glared at him, he grumbled, "Forgive me if I'm not that enthusiastic."

But this time I cared as little about his annoyed look as the others did, given that they'd already counted me in. Flashing a grin at Tony, I said, "Bad news, Mitchell. I'm coming. Deal with it."

The corners of his lips curved up in a stilted grin, and he double-blinked at me. "Oh joy."

Yeah, it would be, for sure...

Before sixth period, Allie finally spilled all the romantic details we'd been waiting for since she'd come to us in the cafeteria. Apparently, Sasha surprised her this morning. She said she'd nearly swallowed her tongue when she'd banged the metal door of her locker shut and seen him standing there. But when he'd told her, "Hey, you do realize I've been chasing you for a while now? I think it's about time you go out with me," she'd been all his. The dreamy look in her eyes made us swoon with her.

While we got dressed after an hour of playing basketball,

ANNA KATMORE

we discussed the camping trip, and I arranged for Susan to give me a ride. Running late now, I rushed out of PE. I had my homework for art in a folder clamped under my arm and hurried to make it to class before the bell rang.

Just as I rounded the last corner, I bumped face first into a much taller guy. I was tossed backward and landed on my ass, my sketches skating a few feet down the corridor.

"Dang! I'm so sorry," I panted, getting on my knees and helping him gather his dropped drawings. "I didn't see you."

He'd squatted, too, and only when I held out a few pictures to him did I notice who I'd actually crashed into. On eye level with Anthony Mitchell. That was a first.

Expecting the worst from him, I tensed, but he remained silent for the second time this week, which freaked me out even more. Swiftly, he'd collected all his drawings, apart from the two I held out to him. His eyes were so wide, they spelled horror in crystal clarity. Slowly, he reached for the drawings.

A soft tug at the sheets in my hand made me look down at them. And then I understood his horror. He probably never wanted me to see those drawings. Or maybe he did, just not now, but a little later, in class, when he could score a fantastic laugh with them. A joke at my cost. The world stopped for a millisecond while I fell out of my dream and face forward into a hole of shock.

"Oh my God," I whispered and dropped from my knees to land on my butt again. My hands shook, my lungs refused to pump enough air in. I was dizzy like I'd been riding too fast on a carousel.

I hated that tears sprang to my eyes, hated that he'd caught me vulnerable like this. But most of all, I hated that he'd used me as a live model for his AVE homework. The female villain he'd chosen to draw was a witch. And apart from being tiny, which showed perfectly because he'd placed her right next to a door where the door knob could easily have poked her eye out, the woman's face bore a striking similarity to what I saw every day when I looked into the mirror. The same features, the same heart-shaped mouth, the same big, dark eyes. Hell, he'd even captured my black hair in a perfect copy. Only this woman had a nose as long as my middle finger, and it was beset with nasty warts that even sprouted hairs. There was an evilness to her eyes that belonged in a Harry Potter movie but not on me. From between her slightly parted lips one rotten tooth peeked out and her hunched back sported a raven that cast the viewer a mean look. The witch clasped a broom with both her clawed hands.

"You—you—" I gasped for air. Letting go of his sketches, I clapped my hands over my mouth, aware that my chest was already rocking with sobs.

The asshole didn't say a single word. He just stared at me like he'd bitten his tongue off.

Close to an emotional breakdown, I watched him shove the pictures into his folder, then his eyes found mine again. I knew he disliked me for a really obnoxious reason, but I'd never dared to believe it was this bad.

A single tear slid down my cheek. "Is…*That* is how you see me?"

The lines of Tony's face hardened. It looked like he was

trying not to grimace. His hand came up to reach for me. Like a snake. Like the enemy. I was lost so deep in hysterics that I felt the urge to hiss at him. Yet all I managed was a trembling gasp as I flinched back. "No...oh my *God!* Just don't touch me!"

He didn't. Instead he clamped his folder under his arm, rose from the ground, and strode into the classroom. As soon as he was gone, some kids helped me gather my sketches, too, but I couldn't appreciate their help right now. I left all my stuff behind and ran in the opposite direction, down the corridor, and outside. With tears coming fast now, my vision got blurry. I stumbled around for a few moments, not knowing what to do or where to go, until eventually I fell to my knees in the grass underneath a wide tree.

I dropped back against the trunk, dragged my legs to my chest, and covered my face with my hands. Every breath burned painfully down my too-tight throat. No way would I go back to AVE now, or ever again.

"Sam?" A concerned but familiar voice made me look up. "What the hell happened?"

Yeah, it was just my luck that Lisa's boyfriend would find me out here, crying like a little whelp. I quickly dabbed at my tears but couldn't say anything to him, so I only shook my head.

"Hey, guys, go on!" he called over his shoulder to a small group of students some twenty feet away. "I'll catch up with you later." Then he squatted in front of me, resting his hands on my bent knees. "Did your cousin give you shit again?"

I could only stare at his face, then my tears spilled over anew.

"Dammit! It's Mitchell." He sighed and dropped to his knees on the dirt, then fished for something in his backpack and eventually handed me a tissue. I cleaned my face with it, then wiped my nose and fought hard to get my sobs under control. Ryan waited in total silence until I had gathered myself and finally stopped crying.

"Wanna tell me what happened so I can knock the idiot's head off?"

His compassion touched me. It almost made me smile. Shoving the tissue into my pocket, I lifted my gaze to the sky and rubbed my palms over my burning hot cheeks. "I saw some of his drawings." My voice was still shaky.

"Okay..."

Looking back at him, I sniffed. "And there was one of me."

"Oh." His eyes widened a bit with surprise, which made me pause. Then he chuckled. "So you saw it, huh?"

My brows knitted together in a skeptical frown. "You think it's funny?"

"In fact, I think it looks quite awesome. So why did that picture make you cry?"

Sorry, what? Did he come to rub salt into my wounds? "Awesome? He made a freaking witch out of me."

Now it was Ryan who looked a bit confused. "A witch?"

"Yes. With a warty nose, hunchback, broom, and all."

"Oh," he said again. Then his lips compressed to a thoughtful line and his dark brows furrowed. "Well, that wasn't the picture I saw of you."

There were more? What was wrong with that guy? It had

only been a stupid glass of club soda and *I* hadn't knocked it over, goddammit! "Why does he hate me, Ryan?" I pleaded.

"He doesn't hate you, Sam. Currently, he's just a little complicated. Your cousin left a deep dent in his bonehead."

"I don't see how that's my fault." I shook my head. "Anyway, I've had enough of his bullshit. Would you tell the others I'm not coming tonight? I'm really not up for the next round."

"It isn't your fault, and he knows it. And no, Sam, you won't cancel on us because of him. Lisa and Susan will never let you. Tony just has to get his shit together like a man, but that's not your problem." Ryan squeezed my knees and his voice turned even softer. "By the way, he's waiting over there." Subtly, he nodded to my left.

I snapped my head around, finding Tony leaning against another tree with what looked a lot like my portfolio clasped in his hands. My stomach tightened into a knot.

"Want me to kick his ass for you?" Ryan asked in a serious tone. "Because if you do, I will. Otherwise, I think I'll leave you two alone. The guy looks like he has something to say."

Thunderstruck, I kept staring at Tony. His face was carved in hard lines, but his eyes didn't hold the usual animosity.

"Okay, I guess that means no ass kicking." Ryan pushed himself up, using my knees. "I'll see you later."

When I looked up at him, he lifted one daring eyebrow, which suggested I shouldn't even think about not showing up. He'd probably come and haul my butt out of the house himself if he had to. No doubt.

Adjusting his backpack on his shoulders, Ryan Hunter walked over to Tony, who pushed away from the tree and looked at the ground. "Seriously, a witch?" Ryan laughed and slapped Tony on the shoulder. "Man...you're such an idiot."

I didn't want Tony to come over to me now that Ryan was gone. I didn't want him to say whatever he had to say. And most of all, I didn't want him to see how my eyes were red from crying. All I wanted was for him to go away.

But he didn't.

Only a couple of seconds later, he was standing right over me. My folder landed next to my boots on the ground.

"You ditched class."

"So? Obviously, you did, too," I replied with the warmth of an Arctic storm.

"Yeah, someone had to bring you your stuff."

"Thanks." My gaze fixed on my knees instead of him, my tone cold and sharp. "Now leave me alone."

Slowly, Tony squatted in front of me, just like his friend had done before. "I will. In a minute."

Right now, a minute with him was an eternity too long. But he'd probably be gone sooner if I kept my mouth shut and let him say whatever he wanted to get out. Besides, my throat was too hoarse to start an argument right now, anyway.

"Listen..."

I did. Yet he paused so long after that single word that I involuntarily glanced up at his face. Heck, he actually looked sorry. And I mean really sorry as in, *I don't know how to make this up to you* sorry.

His tight white tee stretched across his chest as he drew in a deep breath. "I don't know what it is with you, Summers, that draws out the worst in me. It just...*is*."

Oh, wow. If this didn't go down as the most brilliant apology of all time. "Anthony, you turned me into a *witch*." It came out a hoarse whisper.

"I know...That picture should never have gotten into my folder. It was a damn accident."

"The fact that you drew it in the first place was a *damn accident*!" I screamed at his thick skull.

Tony remained calm. "Yeah...that, too." There was a sad note to his tone that I didn't understand and didn't want to either. He continued with a bitter voice. "Look, I know I've given you hell since the day you came through the door of Charlie's. Won't happen again. From now on, I'll stay away from you."

And then he stood and walked off.

I had no intention of going back to class with a face that was red and swollen from crying, so I made my way home.

Pamela, who knew my schedule, looked a bit worried when she saw me coming in through the door. "Is something wrong?"

I should have told her that everything was fine and I just had a little headache, but when she placed her palm on my cheek and asked, "Have you been crying, dear?" I felt my composure slip.

"I just had a really, really bad week," I told her. Then I dropped into one of the high-back chairs in the dining room and buried my face in my folded arms on the table. I expected to hear her soothing voice asking for details, but all I heard was noise in the kitchen. Finally, I looked up and found her sitting next to me. The fruity smell of strawberry tea wafted in my face as she pushed a steaming cup toward me.

For that alone, I decided she was worthy of hearing the details. All of them. Everything about Tony and how he'd made my life hell for no obvious reason. Well, other than that he'd slept with Chloe some time ago and it hadn't worked out for them. And I thought it was pushing it to also tell my aunt about her daughter's bitchy behavior, so I left out that part, too.

"It's really hard to believe that a nice boy like Anthony Mitchell could be so mean to you. And you're sure it has to do with Chloe?"

"So I was told." Again I left out the part where she'd dumped him after sleeping with him.

"But you said he apologized today. I'm sure if he said he'll leave you alone, he will."

"Yeah, maybe." I could only hope so. But with camping tonight, the odds were slim. "By the way, the sleepover I wanted to go to tonight is cancelled. Instead, they invited me to go camping in the woods. Is that okay with you and Uncle Jack?"

"Of course. We should have a sleeping bag for you out in the garage." Pam paused. "You look worried. Do you think Tony will be there, too?"

"I know he will. And it'll be so much fun," I added with a wry glance into my cup. But the anger had already slipped away. With a sigh, I put the tea down and leaned my head against my aunt's shoulder. "Will it always be like this? You know, guys

ANNA KATMORE

being complicated?"

Pam pressed her cheek against my hair. "Er...is that a trick question?" She hugged me tight as we both laughed. "But it will get a little better when they get older, honey."

"When who gets older?" Chloe's voice drifted to us from the kitchen. I lifted my head a split second before she appeared in the doorway to the dining room. Her appalled expression when she saw me in her mom's embrace made the hairs at the back of my neck stand on end. An apple slipped from her hands and dropped to the tiled floor, rolling under the table.

I'd totally missed her coming home. Bad mistake. Quickly, I ducked under the table and picked up the fruit.

Aunt Pamela didn't seem to notice my or Chloe's shock. "We were talking about boys," she told her daughter. "Sam's just discovered how complicated they can be."

"Has she now?" Chloe turned to me and flashed a smile that had nothing to do with friendliness. "So, you're still hanging out with those losers, are you? On second thought, you actually fit right in."

Before I could even suck in a breath to reply, Pam snapped, "Chloe, what in the world has gotten into you?" She pushed herself up with her hands braced on the tabletop. "I don't care for your rude manners toward Sam lately. She belongs to this family, and you will apologize to her this minute."

"What?" Chloe gave a baffled laugh.

"You heard me."

As was to be expected, Chloe didn't apologize, and I didn't really care. But what she said to her mother next took me unaware and shocked me into stunned silence.

"So now you love her more than your own daughter?" My cousin directed a condescending scowl at me. "The little brat that was left on our doorstep? I should have known." She turned on her heel and stormed away.

Pam stood next to me, appalled. She stroked her index finger over her lips, turning from the empty doorway to me and back again. Finally, she said, "I'm sorry, Sam. She didn't mean it."

"Actually, I think she did." It all just added up to a wonderfully miserable day. And though I couldn't understand why, I felt sorry for Chloe. "But it's okay. You should go after her."

Pamela walked to the door then cast me a sorrowful look over her shoulder.

I tried to smile. "Thanks for listening to me, Pam."

TONY

ELBOWS ON MY knees and head resting in my hands, I sat on the bench at the side of the soccer field, staring craters into the grass. I didn't know when I had last felt so shitty. No, that was a lie. I knew exactly when I'd last felt down like this. It was when Hunter and I had fought over Lisa in her room. More precisely, when Hunter had accused me of having slept with Chloe and destroyed my last chance with Liz. While that wasn't exactly the truth, there had been no way to deny that I had royally screwed up.

Right now I wished I could turn back time for a few hours, just like I had wished back then. Mistakes sucked. Especially when I was the one making them and they ended in someone else crying.

How in the world could I have forgotten to take the damn pictures of Samantha Summers out of my folder? I never wanted to hurt the girl like this. But I'd been an asshole to her since the moment I had laid eyes on her. No one of Chloe's inner circle had ever bothered me that much. So why Sam?

Behind me, footsteps were coming closer. I didn't bother to turn around until Hunter slapped me on the shoulder and said, "Man, you fucked this up." He stepped over the bench, planted a soccer ball in the dirt by his feet, and sat down next to me.

"That's all your fault," I muttered.

"Why?" He laughed. "Because it's the second Friday of the month?"

"Because of you I shoved the pictures in the folder in the first place. And after practice I forgot to take them out."

"Oh hey, wait a minute, dude. I did nothing but marvel at them yesterday. No one said to rip the pictures out of my hands."

Yeah right, and let him find out how Samantha Summers had suddenly found her way into almost every picture I'd drawn this week, when I couldn't even explain to myself why that was? Damn, I'd had to do my AVE homework four times until I'd finally managed to sketch a sorceress who didn't have Sam's huge, chestnut eyes or that sweet little nose.

Hunter leaned forward and rested his elbows on his thighs. "How come she saw your drawings, anyway? Did you take them out in class or what?"

"Do I look like an idiot?"

"You want an answer to that?" He lifted a brow at me. I fucking hated when he did that. The girls might go gaga over this shit, but we were guys, goddammit.

"She bumped into me before class, and my stuff scattered across the hall."

"Ouch, that's bad." Hunter paused, then he picked the ball up from the ground and spun it on his fingertips like he was fucking Michael Jordan. "Anyway, in the picture I saw of her, she was doing exercises against a tree. Where was *that* picture? I don't think she'd have collapsed over that one if she'd seen it."

"It was right underneath the one with the witch. I was lucky she didn't pay more attention when she picked them up for me."

"Why not show her? I bet she'd love it. After all, girls are supposed to love being an artist's model."

A sigh pushed up my throat, but it wasn't exactly cool to sigh like a sissy around your soccer buddies, so I growled instead. "She's not my model."

"I think she would be if you let her."

"Why do you think I want her to be?" Then I added in an angrier tone, "And why are we discussing that bungee cord gnome anyway?"

He abruptly stopped spinning the ball and stared at me like I had grown a second head. A grin appeared on his face. "Oh boy, it got you bad."

I liked Hunter. A lot. But sometimes he pissed me off like no one else could. "Oh really, great prophet? What makes you say that?"

Leaning closer in a boy scout-ish, conspiratorial way, he chuckled. "Because you already gave the girl a nickname."

Shit. Had I really? Oh hell, I was so screwed. "That doesn't mean anything."

"It means you like her."

I laughed at that, but I realized I didn't sound as amused as I wished. "You're so fucked up, Hunter. She's just another Summers, and I don't do business with their like." I knocked the ball out of his hands.

He stood and picked it up, then tucked it under his arm as he turned to look down at me. "Hey, little princess, let me tell you something. And you'd better listen up now, 'cause I'm only saying it once. Not every girl is like Chloe Summers, and definitely no other girl is like Lisa. So stop waiting for her, because I don't intend to let her go."

"Yeah, got it," I said through a tight, cynical grin.

"Some *crap* you got. I've watched you turn down about fifteen girls in the past three months. I didn't care, because they were all just nameless chicks. But this one...Sam..." He shrugged. "She's cool. And you know it. She's nice and funny and, whether you like it or not, the girls have decided she belongs in our group."

Where the fuck was Hunter's off button? I hated it when he played big brother around me. "So what?"

He waited a moment, and I feared he'd give me more crap to eat. Instead, he grinned. "So...let's play some soccer." He kicked the ball at me. I ducked and it knocked against the bleachers behind me, bouncing back and landing in the grass again.

"Just you and me?" I asked, picking up the ball and bouncing it on my right knee.

"Yep, you and me. Same goal. To three."

I agreed with a nod and kicked the ball high up in the air. As it zoomed down again, Hunter and I went for it as if it was a matter of life or death. Well, soccer always was for us. Hunter got to it first, but as he headed for the goal, I skated in from the side and smoothly took over. It was my run for the goal now, and the first point should have been a sure-fire thing. Only Hunter crashed into me from the left and knocked me off my feet. Hitting the ground hard, I skittered along in the grass.

"What the hell—"

Hunter scored.

"That was a foul!"

He came over, his fists on his hips. "Who are you going to complain to, little princess?"

I ground my teeth as I got to my feet and dribbled back to the middle of the field. "I get it, we're playing without any rules now."

In round two, I was prepared for his tackling me and blocked an attack with one of my own. But when he went down, he grabbed my ankle and I landed in the dirt with a bellyflop that pressed the air out of my lungs. I rolled onto my back and sat up, glaring at him. "Seriously, *holding my leg*?"

He shrugged it off, then kicked the ball over my head between the posts. "Two, zero!"

Still sitting on the ground, I lifted my arms in surrender, having lost all appreciation for his no-rules game.

Ryan offered to pull me up. "All's fair in love and soccer."

I refused his help but felt the need to smack that stupid grin off his face.

As we went back to the middle to start round three, Hunter placed his hand playfully on my shoulder. "Where's your defense, Mitchell?"

Shot to hell. I grunted at him, taking up a position for the next go. This time he wouldn't get me.

But he scored again, and this time I called him every unholy name I could think of, because he'd taken the ball away from me by ramming his elbow into my stomach.

"Oh, such mean words from a pretty mouth like yours." Hunter laughed at me. "But finally, we get to the point."

Doubling over with my hands braced on my knees and still gasping for air in between cursing him, I spat on the ground then looked up. "And what *is* the point?"

His laugh ebbed into an *I rule* grin. "You're always so touchy when someone breaks through your barriers." He tossed the ball at me. I had to straighten fast to catch it before it hit me in the face.

He gave me a second to make sense of what he'd just said. And, oh my freaking Jesus...

Hunter did that stupid eyebrow thing again, which meant he could clearly hear the bells of my realization. "See you later, little princess. And don't forget to bring your good manners."

I flipped him off and walked to my bike.

ANNA KATMORE

CHAPTER 7

WHILE I PACKED my things for a night in the wild, I tried not to panic at the thought of seeing Anthony Mitchell again after what had happened today. He'd promised to leave me alone, so it could still turn out to be fun.

Yeah right.

I heaved a frustrated sigh. It would all be easier if only I hadn't picked friends from his circle. But dumping Susan, Lisa, and Simone because of him? And even Nick Frederickson? I didn't think so. The guy had grown on me, just like the rest of them.

I stopped in the middle of rerolling the sleeping bag. If Tony insisted on being such a jerk, I'd simply ignore him. He wouldn't get a chance to spoil this weekend for me. Six other friends were coming, so all should be fine. With that decision made, I felt far better and could finally take a deep breath and relax as I finished packing.

Around four, Susan picked me up in a monster that looked strikingly like Mater from *Cars*. Only the two front teeth were missing. "Sorry about this," she said and grimaced. "My mom's car is in the workshop. This is my granddad's. I swear he's just as much a relic as this thing is."

I shrugged, tossed my camping stuff onto the bed of the truck, and climbed into the passenger seat, throwing my hoodie at my feet. "No worries. It's better than strapping all that stuff onto a bike." Afraid the rusty truck would fall apart beneath my ass, I closed the door with caution.

Music from an ancient time sounded from the two speakers in the dashboard. "You like the sixties?" I asked.

"The music's okay. Well, not really. But Grandpa said I can't touch the radio. It's always tuned to this station. You want me to turn it off?"

"Nah. Leave it." It was good for my mood somehow.

With the windows rolled down and the warm wind ruffling our hair, we sang along to "Lollipop", which Susan declared the Sam Summers theme song. After several miles, she took a turn off the highway and continued down a dirt road. This went on for another mile and led to a gravel parking lot by a romantic brook. Parking between a shiny black Jeep and Hunter's dark grey Audi, she cut the engine. "We have to hike from here. It's not far."

Together we climbed out and grabbed the tent, some mats to lie on, and our sleeping bags. It wasn't a long walk, but with all the things we were carrying, I broke into a sweat before we reached the small clearing where everyone was already busy building their tents and setting up a safe firepit.

I tried not to look out for Tony, but my eyes seemed to have a will of their own as they scanned the place for him. Always know where your enemy is, my brain tried to tell me. I found him kneeling in the dirt with his back to us. His white

ANNA KATMORE

muscle shirt exposed bulging biceps as he worked on putting up the bars of his tent.

"Hi, everyone!" Susan shouted.

At that moment, Tony turned to glance at us over his shoulder. I was too slow to look away, and he caught me staring. Even though I tried hard for a blank expression, panic and hate were probably written all over my face. Why the hell couldn't I ignore this guy?

Tony said nothing. Not to me or Susan. But his sheepish gaze locked on mine for several seconds which kind of started to freak me out. In the end, he pressed his lips together a little harder than they already were and returned to his work. *Yeah, I hope you feel awkward, you ass!*

Nick was helping Tony. He smiled when he saw us. Lisa gave a quick wave, then held a metal bar that Ryan was trying to anchor to the ground. Simone shouted, "Hey, guys, what took you so long?"

"We couldn't risk Mater running out of breath, so we had to drive really slowly," I explained.

Simone made a face. "You came in your grandfather's car?"

"Had no choice." Susan shrugged. "It was either that or walk."

We started to set up our tent next to Nick and Tony's. I would have picked a different place, but it seemed this little piece of earth had been saved exclusively for us. We laid out the canvas and sorted though the many thin bars. Unfortunately, this thing came without directions. We were totally lost.

Cross-legged, I sat on the dirt, studied the elements for a

while, and muttered, "Nothing seems to fit anywhere."

"I think we have to stick them together, like into each other," Susan said, holding two bars like chopsticks.

She was right. If you turned them right, the bars slid easily into each other's ends. But after five minutes of slotting them together, we had no idea what to do next.

"Great," I said, eyeing the one long bar we'd constructed. "What do we do now? Bend it into a circle and use it to hang a shower curtain?"

"Either that or we sleep outside." Susan bent the endless line of sticks, making a disappointed face. When she let it go, it snapped back into straight form, lying across our space.

A slim tree branch appeared suddenly in my peripheral vision and pointed to the middle of our bar. "You have to break it up here." Tony's voice came from above me.

What the heck was that? A peace offering? He could shove that right up his ass. I wasn't going to follow any orders from him.

But Susan did. Damn if what he'd said didn't make sense.

"Now you lay them out like a cross and shove them through the loops in the fabric," he explained in a patient voice. What's more, he sounded friendly. Something that was totally new to me—and that I wouldn't tolerate after how he had hurt me.

"Thanks," I grunted. "But I'm sure we can manage alone." Somehow. With lots and lots of time.

"All right." His voice was colder than before. With his hands raised in surrender, he walked away.

And I could breathe again.

Susan and I each held a bar in our hands now, looking at each other. Obviously, she was as clueless as me about what to do next. I hated that I had sent our only help away, but I'd be damned if I worked together with Tony to put up a tent.

"We could make a hammock with these," Susan offered with a grimace and poked her bar into my ribs, which made me laugh. "Or we can just sneak into Lisa's tent while they're sleeping."

Tony cleared his throat behind me. "Simone, would you tell the girls to cross the poles then run the ends into the holes at the corners of the canvas and tie the middle of the tent to the cross?"

A frown creased my forehead. Just before I would have scowled over my shoulder at him I stopped myself. He wasn't worth even a glare.

Simone came over. "Um, girls?" she said in an amused voice, clearly suppressing a laugh. "I think you should run the ends of those into the holes at each corner of the canvas and then tie the middle of the tent to the cross."

"We heard him," I muttered and gave Simone an irritated look.

She shrugged then chuckled as she sat on a cooler, watching us proceed.

Sliding the bars into the holes troubled us a little as we had to lift the middle of the cross at the same time and the fabric strained quite a bit. It was like trying to shove a slippery fish into a loop as small as the nail of my pinky. I cussed under my breath.

Somebody hunkered down by my side and a whiff of masculine shower gel crept up my nose. I turned, looking straight into Tony's eyes. The only reasonable thing would be to tell him to piss off, but the next thing I knew his hands were on mine. In a heartbeat I went stiff, even holding my breath. His hands felt way too warm against my chilled ones.

"Let go," he said in a voice that was both soft and irritated.

I didn't want to. All I wanted to do was shove this idiot out of my way and finish this stupid tent on my own. But with my brain shocked out of functioning, I slid my hands from under his so he could grab the bar instead. I dropped to my butt, scooting a few feet away, and watched him easily thread the bar's end into the designated hole.

Ignoring my bafflement, Tony and Nick worked together to finish setting up our one-night hotel. After a couple of minutes, I eventually managed to rise from the ground and dust off conifer needles and dirt clinging to my butt.

When the boys were done, Tony stopped in front of me, angled his head with tight lips, and arched his brows. It probably translated to something like: *That's how you build a tent, stupid.* It was clear that he didn't expect me to say anything. Probably didn't even want me to. Finally, he walked past me and over to the fire.

"Thank you, Tony!" Susan shouted after him.

He lifted his hand over his shoulder but didn't look back. *"De nada."*

Yeah, right. It totally was *de nada*. Nobody asked for his

help, so thanking him was the last thing I was going to do today. Dammit! Chewing on my lip, I started to help Susan lay out our sleeping bags.

Darkness was setting in by the time we pulled the zipper of the tent closed to join the others around the campfire. Four logs, placed in a square around the fire, served as benches. Ryan straddled one and Lisa sat between his legs, with her back snuggled against his chest. Simone fondled Alex's hair as he laid his head in her lap on another tree trunk. Susan sat down next to Simone. That log was full, and since I didn't want to sit with Lisa and Ryan when they started to make out, I dropped my ass next to Nick on the ground and used the log behind us as a backrest like he did.

A moment later, Tony came out of his tent and sat on the ground in front of the remaining tree trunk. He ripped a package of cheese crackers open, shoving fistfuls into his mouth. He didn't look at me, and I wouldn't look at him either. Instead, I concentrated on the crackling flames.

Nick opened a can of Pepsi which he then passed to me. "Want some?"

The afternoon heat and the struggles with building our quarters had made me thirsty. I took the can with a grateful smile and gulped down half the soda then handed it back to Nick. He sipped from the can and placed it between our hips on the ground.

It didn't take long for Simone to retrieve all the good stuff from the cooler down by the stream. We speared hot dogs on sticks and threw potatoes into the embers at the side of the fire.

Between the sizzling sausages we roasted marshmallows on our sticks.

After we had eaten, a cherry lollipop was a must for dessert. Since I'd come back to Grover Beach, I always carried one with me in my pocket, so I pulled it out and put it in my mouth. A breeze whizzed around the fire, and goosebumps rose on my skin. No one seemed to be bothered by the wind, other than me, sitting there rubbing the chill from my arms. I had yet to get used to the climate in California.

"Are you cold?" Nick asked me.

"Nah, it's okay." I only wished the wind would turn and blow the heat of the fire straight at me. Better to smell like a fried weenie than be shivering when everybody else was warm and comfortable.

Nick scrunched up his face, which looked funny. "I'd offer you a jacket, but I didn't bring one."

"Don't worry. I brought my own." Just not the entire way. Bummer. "It's back in Susan's car. I'll get it later." Or maybe not. A walk through the dark woods alone was so not an appealing idea.

"Hey, want to play truth or dare?" Susan suggested after she'd thrown her stick into the fire and announced that she'd eaten enough to last a week.

"No..." A collective moan came from the guys.

But Lisa and Simone were enthusiastic enough to sway their boyfriends. Even Nick shrugged and gave in eventually. I didn't like this game, because in most cases you had to either verbally or physically embarrass yourself, but I didn't want to be

ANNA KATMORE

a spoilsport, so I agreed. And Tony...well, he had no chance since he was outnumbered.

"I'll go first," Susan exclaimed. "Ryan, truth or dare?"

"Truth," he said after a second.

"Why didn't you hit on Lisa before last summer, when you were in love with her for much longer?"

Lisa tilted her head and smirked over her shoulder at him. "Yeah, Hunter. Why?"

Ryan cut a quick glance to his side, and when I traced it, I found Tony staring into the dancing flames.

"Because she'd been in love with a good friend for eternity," Ryan said then and stroked Lisa's hands on top of her stomach. "It seemed nothing could have dragged her eyes away from pretty boy Mitchell."

We all laughed. Even Tony let a smirk slip.

"Nothing but you," Lisa whispered back to Ryan.

"Truth or dare, baby?" he asked her next.

"I feel brave tonight. Dare."

"I dare you to switch places with me and do what Simone's doing to Alex." He grinned broadly as he rested his head on her lap a moment later.

Brushing her fingers through Ryan's hair, Lisa dared Nick next to jump over the fire. Which he did. And with a ballerina impression, too. It was hilarious to watch, but when he asked me "Truth or dare?" next, I nearly choked on my lollipop.

Afraid he'd make me do something as stupid as fire jumping—I would definitely land in the fire and become toast— I decided for truth.

Nick put a finger to his mouth, looking like he wanted to come up with something really shitty and cruel. But then he smiled, so I knew he was only winding me up. "Okay, what's the meanest thing someone's ever said to you?" he wanted to know.

Damn, I had expected something like *When was your first kiss?* or *Where do you hide the key to your diary?* His question took me unawares and reflexively my glance skated over to Tony. He turned to me, his face expressionless as ever.

After some hesitation, I lowered my gaze to the fire. "Recently, someone called me a hobbit. Probably because of my hair and...because I'm tiny."

Lisa sucked in a shocked breath, but my eyes found their way back to Tony. His brows furrowed as he pressed his lips together, like he always did when he felt—what? Sorry?

"Wow, that is horrible," Nick pointed out the obvious. "Who said it?"

"Doesn't matter," I muttered. It was bad enough that Lisa knew.

"Why? I like *The Lord of the Rings*." Simone only said that because she had no idea of my personal drama going on. She snickered, leaning closer to Susan. "I think Frodo is cute."

Alex pinched her butt. "Come with me into that tent, baby, and I'll give you Frodo."

I dared Susan to pinch Simone again for siding with Frodo when it was an insult about my height, but I smiled so she knew I hadn't taken her comment personally. Simone stuck her tongue out at me, then shrieked when she was pinched once more.

ANNA KATMORE

It was Susan's turn now, and she picked Tony. "Truth or dare?"

"I don't want to pinch Simone's butt, too, 'cause if I did, Alex would rearrange my face." He smirked at Alex, who grinned back. "Truth."

"Truth it is." Susan flashed a crazy look at me through her spectacles which freaked me out, especially as her lips stretched into a broad grin.

Oh boy.

"Let's pretend you have to answer a questionnaire about Sam. Multiple-choice test. First question: Is Sam *pretty* or *ugly*?" Heck, I didn't like how she pronounced the two words. "Would you check the ugly box?"

A breath caught in my throat as the drawing of the witch resurfaced in my mind. I swallowed hard, unable to take my eyes off *that witch* across from me. That was so...*mean*. How could she claim to be my friend and at the same time embarrass me like this? Everyone knew what Tony thought of me.

"I would of course—"

"You know the rules of this game, don't you?" Susan cut his answer short. "If you pick truth and then lie, you'll get the pox and lose all your teeth before you turn twenty-one."

"What?" he and I shot at her at the same time, but then I also started to laugh.

"Who came up with that bullshit?" Tony demanded. He *wasn't* laughing.

"It's common knowledge." Susan sounded dead serious. "Have you never played this game before?" Then she secretly winked at me.

This girl was impossible. But now my heart was beating in my throat as I waited for Tony's answer to fall on my head like a house going down.

When Tony hesitated, everyone turned to him with a curious face. He looked at me briefly, then back at Susan and crossed his arms over his chest. "All right, I wouldn't check the ugly box."

Stop!

Rewind and say that again.

Threatened with the pox, he had just announced that I was *not* ugly? My mouth dropped open. Where had the witch gone? And the hobbit, for that matter.

His head still in Lisa's lap, Ryan smirked at Tony. "There are times when you still surprise me, Mitchell."

"Fuck you, Hunter." Tony cast him a sneer, shoved a handful of crackers in his mouth, and rested his head back on the log behind him. "I don't get what all the fuss is about. She looks okay...so what?"

"So nothing," Susan replied and sent me a conspiratorial smile. "It's your turn, Tony."

I fought to keep my expression calm and under control as we played some more, but the truth was, he'd surprised the hell out of me. I had more than expected him to dismiss the scabies shit and just tell everyone that he thought I looked like a halfling. He was that kind of guy.

With my thoughts still cruising around his last comment, I absently rubbed a chill from my arms.

ANNA KATMORE

Simone leaned forward and asked in a low voice, "Are you cold? You should get your hoodie from Susan's car."

I *was* cold. Really cold by now. But my point hadn't changed at all. "I don't want to wander through the dark alone," I whispered back to her. "I'm afraid I'll never find my way back here."

Alex, whose turn it was to question somebody, heard me and apparently thought it a good idea to make me feel better. He chose Tony, and when he picked dare, Alex said, "I dare you to walk back to the cars with Sam, so she can get her sweatshirt." He flashed a wide grin. "And while you're at it, bring my Gatorade. It's in the middle console of my car."

All muscles in my face gave out. I must have heard wrong. Or so I desperately hoped, as I slowly turned my head to find Tony's bemused gaze on me. Why was everyone suddenly connecting Tony's truths and dares with me?

Tony could have totally ignored the dare—told them he was out of the game and just sat happily by the warm fire. I would have done that. But for the third time since we'd come here, he threw me a curveball.

"Fine." That's what he said.

He got to his feet and disappeared for a moment into his tent, then came out again with a black sweatshirt on and a flashlight in his hand.

Once he had Alex's keys, he headed for the path that Susan and I had hiked to get here. After a few steps he stopped and sent me a stern look over his shoulder. "Are you coming?"

Eyes wide open, I gulped. I cut a pleading glance at Lisa,

but it was Ryan who responded with a subtle nod in Tony's direction. His encouraging smile made me climb to my feet. Slowly. I stepped over Nick's outstretched legs and warily walked toward Tony.

"Sam! Keys!"

The jingling bunch was already flying toward me from Susan's direction when I pivoted, but Tony caught them in front of my face. "C'mon, Summers," he said, and for once, he didn't sound grumpy.

We hiked in silence. He was walking so fast, I nearly had to break into a run to keep up with the small beam of his flashlight. When we arrived at the cars, Tony went for the black Jeep and I tried to work the key into the lock of Susan's ancient vehicle. With no flashlight, I had to feel my way, but once I opened the door, a small light came on overhead and lit the interior. From the floor of the car, I grabbed my hoodie and stuffed my arms into the sleeves as I heard Tony shut and lock Alex's car. I carefully closed Mater's door and locked it.

"I'm ready," I said, turning around. But Tony was gone. Alex's car was dark and deserted. What the hell— "Anthony?" My whisper barely made it past a throat gone dry with fear.

The small light inside Susan's rusty car went out. Pitch-black darkness swallowed everything. A cold shiver ran through me as I froze on the spot.

CHAPTER 8

MY HEART POUNDED in my ears, a loud roar, drowning out the sounds of the gurgling stream nearby. He'd really left me alone. How could he?

"Anthony? Where are you?" I whispered so as not to catch the attention of any mad psycho murderers waiting for me in the woods.

Hell, he couldn't have gone back without me. He couldn't be so cruel.

At that moment, I was painfully reminded of Chloe's display of manners in front of her parents only to later kick me out of her car. Tony knew I was scared, and yet he was playing with me. All the things he had said and done earlier this afternoon, they had only been for show. This was his ultimate joke on me.

As that realization sank in, I damned him to the flaming depths of hell.

A sudden rustling in the trees to my left made my blood run cold. I took a tiny step back, feeling Mater's cold metal behind me. Metal...and something else.

A body.

My heart froze in my chest and I screamed my head off.

Dropping to the ground, I wrapped my arms over my head for protection. As if that would save my sorry ass.

Laughter rang out above me. A sound I hadn't heard before but recognized anyway. I should have been relieved, but I couldn't calm myself. The beam of a flashlight shone in my face shortly before Tony wrapped his fingers around my upper arm and pulled me—still screaming—to my feet.

"You goddamned bastard!" I shouted at him, hammering my fists against his chest. "You complete ass! I nearly peed my pants, you—you—*jerk*!" And if that wasn't embarrassing enough, I started to shake all over.

Tony dodged my slaps, chuckles still erupting from his chest. Then, in a move so fast I didn't see it coming, he grabbed my wrists and twisted me so that he had my back pressed against him in a tight embrace to stop me from hitting him. He mumbled meaningless shit into my ear while I was still firing all kinds of curses at him, trying to get my shock under control. Only when his lips brushed my ear did I go still.

"Shh, Sam, stop it. It's okay. No one's here to hurt you."

I drew in a few deep breaths, struggling to pull myself together as total astonishment rendered me motionless. His arms were around me. And they felt amazingly gentle. His scent of masculine body wash overpowered the smell of conifers and moist grass and settled in my head like a tranquilizer.

I allowed my muscles to relax. He wouldn't hurt me and he hadn't pulled another joke on me. He'd just gone for a second to...*to what?*

"Where have you been?" I croaked.

"Went to pee. I didn't know you'd freak out within ten seconds." There was still a trace of amusement in his voice. I didn't know if I should hate him for it or sink even deeper into his embrace because of it. The feeling was too weird.

As his phone started to ring in his pocket, he released me, bending down for the Gatorade which he handed to me, then fished the phone out and swiped his thumb over the display. "Hey, what's up?" He sounded jolly again, as he spoke into the phone. "Nah, she's just a little jumpy. Everything's fine," Tony assured whoever and hung up, then tucked the phone back into his pocket.

In the beam of the flashlight that now came from the ground beneath us, I nailed him with a death glare. "Never. Do. That. *Again!*"

"What? Hug you or scare you?" he teased. Then he added, "For someone your height, you actually have a powerful punch, Summers." Rubbing his sternum, he grimaced. "Let's go back. They're worried I lost you in the woods."

"They heard me?" I whined.

"All of Grover Beach probably heard that scream." He picked up the flashlight from the ground, then wrapped his fingers briefly around my upper arm and made me move.

When he let go again, I rubbed the spot, which quickly grew cold. Gee, he'd touched me. I rolled my eyes at myself. But the big deal was that he did it by choice, with no gagging sounds but instead a small smile.

Was this his way of making up for being such a dickhead? I couldn't quite believe it, but if it was, I certainly wasn't going to complain. I liked this Tony much better than the asshole I'd gotten to know the past few days.

He walked slower than before, so I didn't have to run to keep up with him. It seemed he wasn't in a hurry to get back. And with this new side of him shimmering through, neither was I. But my wariness still lingered.

"So, is *this* you 'staying away from me'?" I asked.

"I honestly intended to," he confessed in a low voice. "But with those *awesome* friends of mine, you see how that's impossible."

Oh. So nothing had changed in the end. "I'm sorry they forced me on you, Anthony," I muttered, feeling like...well, frankly, I didn't know what to feel at all tonight.

Tony threw his head back, sighing, obviously exasperated. "Good Lord, would you stop calling me Anthony already? You sound like my gran."

"You told me to call you that." And it was *not* a nice memory.

"Yes, I did. And now I'm telling you to stop. My name is Tony." Then he halted and spun me around to him. "And you don't have to be sorry. I didn't say I didn't want you to come along, did I?"

"Umm...I guess not." My eyes grew wide as he planted his hands on my shoulders. I took a small step back.

"So why don't we just—"

Unfortunately, I didn't hear the rest of it, because the small step backward took me over the edge of the riverbank. With a shriek, I lost my footing, tumbled down the small slope, mowing

ANNA KATMORE

down the weeds, and landed with a splash on my butt in the middle of the stream. Gasping and sputtering, I felt the cold water seep into my clothes, but I couldn't move for what seemed like forever.

"Sam?" Tony's anxious voice drifted down to me. The beam of the flashlight traveled systematically around me until it was pointed straight at my face. "Are you hurt?"

I shook my head, totally perplexed.

Because the light was blinding me, I couldn't see his face, but his sudden laughter traveled through the woods. "Oh my God. Would you please get out of there?"

Yeah, like I enjoyed sitting in the cold water. The jet of light jumped about as he made his way down the small slope, then he leaned forward, grabbed my hand, and hauled me to my feet. Water dripped from my clothes and my boots had filled up to the brim.

Tony helped me out of the brook and back up to the path. My teeth clattered. I shivered violently. "I—I lost Alex's Gatorade."

"Don't worry. I'm sure he'll survive the night without it." Tony squeezed the flashlight between two twigs of a bush and left it there with the light pointed at us. "Strip," he ordered and pulled his sweatshirt over his head. The muscle shirt underneath traveled up over his rippling abs with it, but he adjusted the fabric a moment later.

I stood stiff like the snowman I'd started to become and stared at him with my mouth open.

"What are you waiting for?" Tony asked.

A nervous laugh escaped me. "I'm not g-g-getting naked."

"Oh yes, you are. You're wet to the bone. If I bring you back with pneumonia, the others will never let me live it down. So off with your hoodie and shirt." Then something appeared on his face that I hadn't seen there ever before. A teasing smile. "You can leave your pants on."

I probably looked like I'd been hit by a stunning spell.

Getting impatient, he reached out and unzipped my hoodie. I sucked in a breath, but in fact I was too cold to object to anything right now. Until he shoved the hoodie down my arms and grabbed the hem of my T-shirt next.

"Stop!" I caught his wrists with my ice-cold fingers.

He waited.

"All right," I murmured. "I'll take it off, but you t-turn around." He didn't have to see the silly Snoopy bra I was wearing tonight.

"Of course." With a glance skyward, Tony spun around and draped his hoodie over one shoulder for me to grab when I was ready.

I yanked off the wet tee and tossed it over his other shoulder, which made him cringe and whine—and made me smile. When I put on his sweatshirt, I had to roll up the cuffs three times to make my hands appear. Oh damn, did it feel good. Cozy, warm, and... "Oh my *God*, I didn't know you actually smelled so good!" I teased him by sniffing his collar as he turned around again.

"I do take showers every once in a while, you know," he replied. Then he looked at me for a couple of silent seconds and

ANNA KATMORE

whatever he saw there made him grin. Finally, he grabbed the flashlight and pulled the hood of his sweatshirt playfully over my head.

We strolled back side by side, with him carrying my wet things. In spite of it only being a small act of gentleness, it didn't escape me. However, while Tony's hoodie kept me warm on top, my legs and feet started to get numb. The thought of the fire was the only thing that kept me walking.

As we reached the campsite and the squeaking of my drenched boots announced our arrival, everyone turned their heads. Lisa gasped at the sight of me, Ryan jerked up from his lying position, and Susan jumped to her feet and dashed over to us. "What in the world—"

"She fell into the brook," Tony broke her off with a dry tone. "And don't you look at me like that, Miller. I didn't push her."

"One can never tell with you," Susan growled. "Are you all right, Sam?"

"Yeah," I told her through a grimace. "Just wet from the waist down and awfully cold."

She let me pass, and I hurried to the campfire. The first gush of warmth that hit me in the face coaxed out a moan from me that made everyone laugh. I hunkered by the fire with the hood still up, holding my hands over the blaze. Ah, flaming heaven.

Tony told the others some vague details about my misstep and how I ended up sitting in the stream. I only listened with one ear, the comfortable warmth engrossing me entirely. After a while, I folded my arms around my bent legs. Rocking gently back and forth on my heels, I laid my cheek on my knees.

With my head tilted like this, my gaze landed on Tony, who sat in front of his former log again. We looked at each other for a couple of seconds while the rest talked about something else—soccer, as usual.

Tony said in a very low voice, "Take off your boots."

He was right, I needed to get out of them. I knew from my dad that keeping wet shoes on for longer than a few hours could do serious damage. I wanted to keep my feet healthy, so I unlaced my boots and slipped my feet out, placing the boots so that the fire could dry the insides. My socks soon followed. That's when I noticed my left foot was smeared with blood dripping from an injury on my shin. Rolling up my pant leg, I inspected the wound. It was a nasty cut about two inches long. Numbed from the cold, I hadn't felt any pain. But it looked like it needed stitches.

I cut a quick glance around to make sure no one had noticed what had happened to my shin, then I rolled my pant leg back down. Maybe it wasn't that bad after all. A pretty little Band-Aid was probably enough to fix it. But whatever the wound needed, it would have to wait until tomorrow. A small cut wasn't worth destroying everyone's evening.

Twenty minutes later, my pants were as dry and warm as if they'd just been ironed on me. Only they smelled like burning wood, as did the rest of me. I slipped into my still-damp boots to hide the blood on my leg from the others before I rose from my comfortable spot by the fire and went looking for my tee and

ANNA KATMORE

hoodie. Totally forgotten, they hung over Tony's log with no chance to dry.

"Crap," I mumbled, gathering them up.

Tony's gaze moved to the wet bundle in my arms then back at my face. "Keep my hoodie on tonight."

I really didn't want to, but I knew I was smiling right then. Mostly as a response to the corners of his compressed lips lifting slightly. I accepted with a single nod, then followed Susan into our tent as everyone else said good night and went to sleep, too. With my pants and Tony's sweatshirt still on, I crawled into my sleeping bag, zipping it up to my chin. The light of the small fire we'd left burning shone through the tent, making shadows dance on the walls.

"Did you have a nice time?" Susan whispered next to me.

I tilted my head toward her. "Mm-hm."

"So you're happy you came with us?"

The summary of the evening was that Tony and I had made peace, he'd called me *not ugly*, and I was wearing his sweatshirt right now. Some progress after a terrible start, I'd say. "Yes," I whispered back.

A wide grin crept to Susan's lips. "Welcome to the Bay Sharks, Sam."

I knew what she meant by it. Everyone had welcomed me into their small circle of friends from the very first day. But it had never felt whole until tonight, when the last of them had let me in, too. "Night, Susan," I said and snuggled deeper into the sleeping bag, wrapped in a cloud of Tony's body wash.

Hard to say how much time had passed when a burning

pain in my leg tore me from a dreamless sleep. I buried my face into the crook of my arm to choke back a gasp.

The cut troubled me over the next couple of hours. Sleep was a thing of the past. I didn't want to turn on the flashlight and wake Susan, who was snoring happily in her sleeping bag, and the fire had gone out by now, so I was trapped in the pitch-black night. I tried not to whine as the pain grew worse.

When dawn finally crept through the woods, I sneaked outside, slowly going insane with the thumping pressure on my leg.

Closing the zipper as quietly as possible, I left a sleeping Susan in the tent. Then I tiptoed away from the campsite. I didn't expect anyone to be up this early, so I was startled to find Ryan leaning against a tree down by the stream and Tony lying sprawled in the grass, quietly chatting.

When Ryan spotted me, a puzzled look appeared on his face. Tony tilted his head back and saw me, too. "Good morning," they both said in low voices.

"Ugh, hi." I shifted uneasily, hoping they wouldn't notice the huge spot of dried blood on my pants. "How long have you guys been up?"

"Only a few minutes," Ryan said. "Why are *you* up so early?"

"I—er..."

Suddenly Tony rolled around to his stomach, a scowl on his face. "Is that blood on your leg?"

"Um...no."

"Of course it is." He got to his feet and walked up the

ANNA KATMORE

grassy slope. Ryan followed, and they both made me sit down on the ground, urging me to show them my leg.

"Ah, seriously, it's...um..." Goddammit, I needed to stop this silly stuttering, and fast.

Ryan lifted a questioning eyebrow. "It's *nothing*, you're trying to say?"

"Just a scratch, no big deal."

He tried to shove my pant leg up, but the garment was stuck to my skin with dried blood and I winced. "This isn't *nothing*," he argued with a scolding edge to his voice and started working the fabric gently away from the wound. "Did this happen when you fell into the brook?"

I swallowed hard and nodded.

"Why didn't you tell us?" Tony snarled.

"I didn't want to ruin everybody's evening."

Tony rolled his eyes, and the next moment a sharp pain ripped through me. Ryan had yanked the leg of my pants up. The wound had come free. I almost choked at the sight. He was right. This seriously *wasn't* nothing. It looked ugly. Blood mingled with dirt, and some sort of substance seeped out of the wound.

"Oh my freaking *eew!*" Tony exclaimed.

Ryan lifted his head to him. "Is there some bottled water left?"

Tony nodded and was gone before I could tell them I didn't want anybody to mess around with and possibly butcher my leg. When he came back, I covered the injury with my hands. "Nobody's going to touch this," I warned in a voice gone lethal.

With a hand on my shoulder, Tony squatted down beside us. "It's all right. Hunter knows what he's doing. He's the son of a vet."

I gave them both an incredulous look. *"Excuse me?"*

Laughing, Ryan moved my hands away. "Don't worry. Mitchell's just being silly. But I've patched myself up more times than I can remember. Trust me, I do know what I'm doing." He unscrewed the bottle and slowly poured the water over my seeping wound.

It burned like a thousand needles being pierced into my shin. I sucked a breath in through my teeth, and again when he wiped the sides of my leg clean with a tissue that Tony had brought, too. When most of the dirt was washed away, it didn't look so bad anymore. Just a vicious red cut deep into my flesh. And from the middle protruded a large splinter of wood.

Oh. My. God. I trembled as weakness invaded me. An eerie shiver ran down my spine.

Both boys looked at each other, then at me. "You know this has to come out, Sam," Ryan said in a voice that held compassion but also determination.

Yeah, a Band-Aid alone wouldn't do any longer. Moaning, I rubbed my hands over my face. "I don't even know where the doctor is in this town."

"The doc's not on duty and it's twenty miles to the next hospital," Tony told me wryly.

Ryan still had his hand on my calf as he turned to Tony. "Take her to my dad?"

Tony glanced at his watch. "It's five fifteen."

"It only takes a call. I'll wake Lisa and tell her we're going."

"Let the girls sleep. I can take Sam to your house."

"Hey, stop it, both of you," I interrupted them. "I'm not going to have an animal doctor cut something out of my leg."

Ryan squeezed my calf a little tighter and gave me an encouraging look. "I promise you he won't cut anything. But it needs some sterile tools to get that out. I would hate to peel this out with just my fingers. However," he drawled, placing his thumbs on the outer edges of my wound and pulling it slightly apart, "if you prefer that, I can—"

"No-ho!" I cut him off and shoved his hands away. His smirk revealed that he'd never intended to get the splinter out with his bare hands. I sighed. "All right. I'll go see your dad."

"Good." Ryan nodded and punched a button on his phone. Probably his parents on speed dial. "Hey, Dad," he said after what seemed an eternity. "My friend hurt herself last night, and now there's a piece of wood stuck in her shin. Can you take a look at it?" He paused a second. "No, not Lisa. Her name's Sam. Tony will be home with her in twenty minutes." He nodded at Tony, who got to his feet and pulled me up, too.

"Come on, Summers. Let's get you patched up," he said while Ryan finished his call.

We headed back to the campsite, where I slipped into my boots and Tony fetched his car keys from inside his tent. Two minutes later, we were on our way out of the woods, me limping and Tony casting me worried sideways glances.

TONY

"WEIRD DAY, YESTERDAY, huh?" I said in a low voice as I walked the bungee gnome through the woods toward my car. I just had to say something. She was too silent, and it made me feel uncomfortable.

She tilted her head, arching one eyebrow.

I slowed down a little, because she was limping badly with her injured leg and I didn't want to give her any more trouble. "First I made you cry, then I rescued you from the river..."

At that she laughed out loud. "You didn't rescue me! I was sitting in water that barely reached my chest."

"Yeah, but you're tiny," I taunted her, feeling strangely attracted to the sound of her laughter. "The current could have easily swept you away."

"Shut up!" She swatted my arm and pulled a face, but a quick smile tugged at her lips. Did that make us friends?

Suddenly, I remembered I didn't care for another Summers in my circle of friends and tamped down at the stupid happiness in my chest that had started to grow since I had first seen her this morning.

Three trees farther down the path, Sam cleared her throat. "Tony, can I ask you something?"

I liked that she'd called me Tony instead of Anthony, but at the same time I wondered if it had been a mistake to tell her to do so. It meant I'd already let her into the friend zone, and to shove her out again was going to be a hard job. "What's up?"

"It certainly wasn't just the spilled water that pissed you off. Will you tell me why you've hated me from the beginning?"

I sighed and deliberated how much of the truth I could tell her and still be safe. None, I eventually decided, so the only thing she got out of me was a tight smile. "No."

"Must be something terrible if it made you turn me into a witch," she muttered.

Thank God, she had no idea what else I'd turned her into. "Don't look so frustrated, bungee. Too much info will just give you a headache."

"Bungee?"

I stiffened. "What?"

"You just called me 'bungee'." Her eyes narrowed as she stopped and folded her arms over her chest. "What is that? A new insult?"

My breath turned to ice in my lungs. I couldn't really have just called her that out loud. What the hell was wrong with me?

"And here I thought we were past all that crap," she grumbled and limped on, leaving me behind. "My bad."

I caught up with her fast. "It wasn't an insult, Summers." Pulling the hood of my sweatshirt—which Sam was still wearing and which looked annoyingly hot on her—up and over her eyes, I gave her a playful shove against her shoulder. Not a hard one, just a gentle push, but she stumbled anyway and whined.

"Oh shit!" Reaching for her arm, I steadied her.

Soft laughter disrupted her whining. What—she was fucking with me? That little troll! Oh well, I probably deserved that for everything I'd done to her. Most of all for making her cry. But still. I pulled her closer to my side with a firm grip on her upper arm and snarled a threat in her ear. "I should dump you in that brook again, wench."

"Have more clothes to share?" she asked, her tone teasingly sweet.

I couldn't stop myself from imagining her in my white muscle shirt instead of that hoodie. Shaking the riveting thought out of my mind, I let go of her arm.

CHAPTER 9

I CLIMBED INTO Tony's dark red Toyota, still not sure what to make of this strange morning and our even stranger conversation. Were we about to become friends? Tony could be seriously cute when he wanted to be, with a very nice smile. It just took him so long to show it.

But I wasn't sure if that was enough to make up for all the shit he'd given me this week.

Anyway, I didn't want to think about that now. First, I needed to get rid of that nasty little piece of wood in my shin. It hurt like hell and it looked even worse. I chewed on the inside of my cheek, trying to extinguish one sort of pain with another. It didn't work.

Tony had been quiet for most of the walk through the woods and still was now while he drove us to Ryan's place. I wished he'd say something. Talk to me, to distract me from my aching leg. He could even call me all sorts of tiny right now, if only he wouldn't be so closed off again.

From the rearview mirror hung a short chain and on it dangled a picture in a plastic frame. I reached out to hold it still and took a closer look. It was of a happy couple with a much younger edition of Tony Mitchell between them.

"You must be quite the family guy to have this in your car," I said, fishing for a conversation starter.

"It's not my car, it's my mom's," he answered as I let go of the small frame. "I'm hoping to get my own car before Christmas. That's why I'm bussing tables at Charlie's." There was a cold note to his voice as he cut a quick glance at me.

I wondered if he expected me to slag off his job. Chloe would probably do it. I wasn't going to. "That's really cool of you to work for your car. Not many students would do that." Definitely not my cousin.

"I don't have a choice. My parents won't give me presents as huge as a vehicle." He snorted, and there was a small hint of frustration in it. Then a grin followed. "But they will double whatever I make, so I guess I could be much worse off."

"Yeah, you could be," I seconded, giving him a wry smile when he looked at me briefly before taking a left turn onto a very familiar road. "For instance, if you had to rely on your weird cousin to lend you hers."

Tony chuckled at that. I was sure if anyone in the world knew what I meant, it was him. "You don't get along with her?" he wanted to know as he drove up the road that led to Chloe's house.

"We used to get along really well. But something seems to have changed. And it's not me." I shifted in the seat, a little uncomfortable. "Anyway, why are you driving me home? I thought we were going to see Ryan's dad." Scaring Pamela out of her bed at six in the morning didn't seem like a good idea to me.

ANNA KATMORE

"We are. Hunter lives not so far from your family. Just a few streets up."

Oh.

When we passed my aunt's house, I felt the urge to scoot lower in the seat while throwing a tentative glance out the window and up to the second floor where Chloe's room was.

"What are you *doing* down there?"

I lifted my head to Tony's confused voice and only then realized just how deep in the seat I'd moved. I straightened, clearing my throat. "Um, nothing."

He laughed. "Bullshit. You're hiding! Why?"

I cut one last glance over my shoulder. When we were well out of sight of Chloe's window, I relaxed. "That's too weird to tell."

"Random guess...she doesn't like you hanging out with us," he said, then added as an afterthought, "or with me in particular."

I gaped at him because I didn't know what to read in his amused voice.

"So, she was nicer in the past?" Tony asked after a few seconds of silence. "I would have liked to get to know *that* personality."

"That ship has sailed," I grunted. And then I wondered if they would still be together if they had met sooner, when Chloe had still been Chloe and not the Barbie Clone.

Tony surprised me when he asked, "What's so funny?"

"Hmm? What?"

"You're grinning. Why?"

Oh. I hadn't realized I was. "Just something that Simone—or Lisa—recently called my cousin."

Tony turned his head to me and lifted one eyebrow together with the corners of his mouth. "Barbie Clone?"

"You know about that?"

"Of course. Lisa used to give me shit about it. It was her favorite term when she talked about Chloe."

Since Tony seemed open for conversation right now, I thought it was a good moment to test my luck some more. "You were a couple...you and Chloe?"

His face immediately hardened. But he granted me an answer...after an uncomfortably long minute of thinking. "Not a couple. But we dated."

"It must have been some intense dating. Even my aunt remembers you." I rolled my eyes. "She said you were *such* a sweet boy." Shit, could I never stop my damn mouth from getting me into trouble? And I would undoubtedly get the bill for it in just a moment.

"You talked to your aunt about me?"

At his surprised tone, I lowered my chin and gazed at my knotted fingers. "Um, yeah. I told her what a jerk you actually were."

Heartfelt laughter filled the inside of the car. "All right. I can see that." Tony stopped the car in front of an impressive mansion and cut the engine. "Get out. We're here."

I ogled the front of Hunter's house through the windshield. Wow. And I'd thought my uncle's house was huge. But this...one could only hope to be given a map upon entering.

ANNA KATMORE

The car door opened and tore me out of my stunned gazing.

"Need an extra invitation, Summers?"

I looked up, grinned, and climbed out. As I put weight on my injured leg, I was reminded of the biting pain and limped after Tony. We didn't have to ring the bell because the door opened as we climbed the steps.

A woman with warm brown eyes just like Ryan's smiled at us. Her hair was fair like that of an angel, but she was unmistakably his mother. "Tony, dear, where have you been all this time? I haven't seen you in weeks," she exclaimed and kissed him on the cheek.

"I have a job now, Jessie." Tony beamed at her, squaring his shoulders like a confident preschooler. It made me giggle.

"I heard that. Ryan told me, and I ran into your mother the other day. She's very proud of you." Mrs. Hunter cupped Tony's cheek briefly with her hand, then she released him and turned to me, extending both her hands to grab mine. "And you must be Samantha. I'm Jezebel. Come in, dear. My husband is already waiting for you in his practice."

I hardly had time to say hello before she dragged me into a warm and cozy home that I would have never expected from the outside. Tony led the way past a long set of winding stairs, into the back of the house. Limping, I hurried after him, so as not to lose him in a place as big as a football stadium.

Through a wide door we entered a different part of the house that smelled strongly of cat food and disinfectant. It was painted in clean white, the floor tiles off-white, and the many spotlights in the ceiling cast a way-too-bright light for six o'clock in the morning. We walked through two more rooms, one lined with all sizes of boxes and carriers, where cats and dogs slept the morning away, and another room resembling a sterile kitchen. Bandages, syringes, and tubes filled many cabinets and chests.

Behind the next door, we were greeted by a tall man whose black hair had already started to gray at the temples but who was otherwise a perfect Ryan Hunter replica—give or take a few wrinkles around his eyes, and of course the glasses.

"Tony," he said, shaking Tony's hand.

"Good morning, James. This is my friend, Sam." Tony nodded at me. "She was a little clumsy last night."

I knew this was the wrong moment to dwell on it, but had he really just called me a friend? At my puzzled look, Tony narrowed his eyes at me as though he knew exactly what was on my mind and was testing the term for himself. Eventually, he shrugged it off and let Mr. Hunter step forward to shake my hand.

"Hello, Sam, I'm James Hunter. Ryan said there's a piece of wood in your leg. Come over here and let me take a look." He ushered me over to make myself comfortable on some sort of cold metal table in the middle of the room that was clearly for animals and not for people.

I guessed it was fine to just sit and not lay back.

Taking off my boot and rolling up my pant leg, I was getting really uneasy. Not because a vet was inspecting my leg, but because of the nasty silver scalpel in his hand as he did.

"Do you think I need stitches, sir?" I asked him, frowning

ANNA KATMORE

at my leg.

"Hmm." He grabbed a pair of latex gloves from his coffee-brown desk, which dominated one half of the room, put them on, and tested the little splinter with his index finger. Biting my bottom lip, I strangled a whine in my throat at the immediate pain.

"Probably no stitches, Sam, but it's going to hurt a little when I work this fragment out." Mr. Hunter grimaced. "I'm not authorized to give you a local anesthesia. So if you'd rather have this done by a specialist, I can give Doctor Decker a call and send Tony over to Pismo Beach with you."

I didn't know where that place was and I preferred not to wait any longer to get the splinter out. It already hurt like hell—it couldn't hurt much worse to have it removed. "No, please do it."

He nodded and moved to get a few things: a big plastic syringe filled with clear liquid, some pads, a pair of tweezers, and a bandage. While he was placing all these things next to me on the metal table, Tony bent forward to inspect my weeping wound.

"Wicked..." His face screwed up with disgusted awe, but when he looked up and found me watching him with growing horror, he quickly put on an encouraging—however faked—grin. "It isn't that bad."

I cast him a wry glance. "Yeah right. I wonder if you'd say the same if this piece of wood was stuck in *your* leg instead."

"Don't worry, Sam," said Mr. Hunter. "It'll be over in a minute. Let me just clean the wound first." He held up the big plastic syringe and grabbed a pad from the small stack he'd brought. Then he had me place my foot on the table and bend my knee, so he had better access.

I was prepared for a lot, but not for the biting, mind-shriveling pain that spread through my shin the moment he let some of the liquid drip into the wound.

"Holy crap, what's— Oh my *God*! Bloody *fuck*!" Screaming, I jumped off the table, because I didn't know what else to do, and half hopped, half limped erratically around the room. Teeth clenched, I grunted more curses and bent over, then dipped against the wall, where I finally dropped to my ass with my back sliding down the cold tiles. I sucked air in through my nose, my teeth gritted so tightly I could hear crunching noises inside my jaw.

Tony watched me with obvious interest, while Mr. Hunter seemed a little more concerned. Thank God the burning started to ease a few seconds later, so I could breathe normally again. "Shit. That *hurt*!"

"Do you still want me to remove the splinter without anesthesia?" the doctor asked warily.

I could only hope that the disinfectant was the worst part of the procedure. I nodded but felt my heart slip to my pants. However, I was in a room with two men. I wouldn't turn tail.

Tony came over to me and grabbed my hand, pulling me to my feet. "Come on, Summers. Don't play the weak sissy here. I know you're harder than that."

In spite of my misery, he managed to make me laugh. As he helped me back to the metal table, I had time to thoroughly

ANNA KATMORE

feel his biceps while holding on to his arm. It didn't only look stone hard, it actually was. And his skin felt warm and smooth.

"Nice arm, Mitchell," I teased him, stroking my fingers down the inside of his biceps, but it was probably more to distract myself than to compliment him.

Tony chuckled. "Having fun down there, Summers?" He didn't shake my hand off.

"Yeah. If nothing else, you're *some* distraction." I stuck my tongue out at him.

Mr. Hunter helped me back onto the examination table. "Are you ready?" he asked with an encouraging smile.

"Yeah. I guess." I could hardly let the wood grow roots inside me, right? But when he bent forward to grab the splinter with the tweezers, I winced even before he could pinch it and pulled my leg away.

With cheeks reddened by shame, I quickly brought my foot back into place. "Sorry, I didn't mean to do that."

He looked a bit uncertain. "Shall we wait another moment, Sam?"

"No, no. I'm fine. Really. Just go on." I waved my hands, encouraging him to proceed.

Mr. Hunter pinched the splinter with the pair of tweezers, but I didn't let him pull it out just yet. I couldn't do anything about it—my courage seemed to have gone for a drink...without me.

"No! Damn. Please. *Wait!*" The words shot out at random from my mouth and I covered my wound as soon as he let go of the wood in my flesh. "Maybe...I don't know. Perhaps we should just wait until...until it falls out by itself?" My voice sounded whiny. Way too desperate.

James Hunter had mercy on me and didn't push me to let him butcher my leg. Contrary to Tony. He sat down next to me and leaned closer to my ear. "Get your shit together, Summers. This will be over in a second. And you know as well as I do that this fucking splinter won't *fall out*." He leaned back so I could see his smirk. "If you want, you can feel my muscles for distraction again. Or I can feel yours." He didn't hesitate to squeeze my upper arm. "Ah, no muscles there," he announced with a playful pout. "You're weak. Just like I expected."

I shoved him hard from the metal table. "That'll teach you to call me weak," I scolded him with a smile.

"Right. I forgot, you're the strongest of the seven dwarfs." He rubbed his chest as though I had done serious damage, and this time his teasing about my height didn't bother me at all. It was clear he was winding me up for a reason. While my thoughts had gone astray, Mr. Hunter had seized the opportunity to catch the splinter again and was ready to pull it out.

I shook my head at him, fighting against a raising panic. "I know Tony is trying to distract me, because you think I won't feel the pain then. But this won't work. I *will* feel it. And it *will* hurt! Can't you just give me one of those shots for dogs or cows to numb my leg?" I whined.

Tony lifted his brows dubiously. "For cows? Seriously, Summers? That would knock you out for days."

"I'm fine with that."

ANNA KATMORE

"And why do you think my distracting won't work? I think I'm pretty good at it."

I felt the doctor's hand squeeze my calf tighter to hold me in place, but I had to answer Tony before I could tell the doctor to leave my leg alone. "No, you aren't. In fact, you suck."

"Really?" He reached for my hand and at the same time grabbed something from Mr. Hunter's stuff that lay on the metal surface. "So what's this?" Holding the small aerosol can just a couple of inches away from my skin, he must have triggered it, because in the next instant I felt a weird sensation of ice-cold spray on the back of my hand...and a stinging pain in my shin.

"Whoa, what are you doing?" I shouted at both of them in shock and pulled my hand and leg away.

Tony flashed a fabulous toothpaste-commercial grin at me while Mr. Hunter held out a piece of wood the size of a freaking toothpick between the tweezers.

"You—you tricked me!"

"And aren't you glad we did?" Tony asked, the grin still perfectly in place.

I made a sullen face. But in the end, I was happy the splinter was out, whatever way they'd done it. Resting my forehead on my bent knee, I closed my eyes and exhaled a long breath.

A gentle hand squeezed my shoulder. I thought it was the doc, but a moment later, Tony said way close to my face, "Well done, Summers."

I turned my head and found him sitting opposite me on the table.

"I didn't know you were capable of hiding half a tree inside your leg," he taunted with a wink.

The splinter was far longer than I'd expected. Of course it would hurt like heck. "Maybe I should keep it as a souvenir. To always remind me of the day that Anthony Mitchell called me a friend and not a plague." I flashed a mocking smile, but a moment later I flinched back as Mr. Hunter had another go at my wound.

He cleaned it once more before putting a bandage on my leg. "It looks all right to me now, but I want you to change the dressing every evening and then come back to me in three days for another look."

I nodded. The Hunters were almost neighbors. It shouldn't be too hard to find my way back here. I shook his hand and told him thanks before Tony and I left his practice through a different door than we'd come in. We walked back to Tony's car, but when he unlocked the doors, I hesitated to get in.

It was a walk of only five minutes back to my aunt's house, and I could easily do that now with my leg neatly wrapped up in a bandage. I also didn't want to be a burden on Tony any longer, even if the morning with him had been astoundingly nice—apart from the pain and all.

A thought crossed my mind. If we really were on the road to becoming friends, he'd probably insist on giving me a ride home anyway, no matter what I said. Just like back in the woods when he and Ryan hadn't let me back out of getting my leg tended to. So this could be my ultimate test.

"What's up?" Tony demanded, disrupting my thinking,

ANNA KATMORE

already one foot inside the car and one hand on the steering wheel.

"Nothing. I think I can walk home from here. It's not far really."

Tony gaped at me for a second, then he turned his head to look down the road and back at me. His forehead creased. "You sure?"

Was I? "Umm, yes. It's no big deal."

"All right." He shrugged. "I guess I'll see you Monday in AVE then." He lowered into the driver's seat, shut the door, and the engine came alive.

I waited for him to roll down the window and prompt me to get into the car so he could drive me home after all. But the window never moved. Tony steered away from the curb and the Toyota swiftly became a small red dot as it sped away from me.

"Okay..." I mumbled, staring after him. Obviously, the road to our friendship had ended in front of Hunter's house.

CHAPTER 10

SHORTLY BEFORE SEVEN o'clock on Saturday morning, I slipped through the front door of my current home. I expected no one to be up just yet, but Pamela was out of bed already, and I joined her in the kitchen to have a cup of tea and toast. When she caught me limping, I told her about the escapade with the river and the splinter in my leg and that I had met James Hunter, the vet.

After her initial worry about my accident, she was glad to hear that Tony and I had found a base to move on from, especially after my breakdown yesterday. She caressed my hair. "See, nothing is ever as bad as it looks at first sight."

I could only laugh about that. "Well, the thing with Tony still looked bad after a week."

"Some guys are just a little slower with opening up. It's the result that counts. And if he drove you to Jimmy Hunter's, he seems to be just the boy I remember."

Yeah, maybe.

We didn't sit alone for long, because my uncle joined us then in his pajama bottoms and a white T-shirt, his hair standing at crazy angles. I hadn't seen Uncle Jack like this in...well, I had *never* seen my uncle this way before. He looked out-of-his-mind tired, and grumpy wrinkles gathered around his eyes.

"Good morning, Sam," he grumbled, sounding as worn out as he looked.

As he got a mug and poured himself a cup of scalding coffee, I leaned into Pam. "What's the matter with him?"

"He was up most of the night trying to find his Constantin," she replied, whispering like me.

"His what?"

"His Vacheron Constantin. His black watch, it was really expensive. He took it off yesterday after work, but when he went to put it on again after showering, he couldn't remember where he'd left it."

Jack sipped his black coffee, glaring at Pam over the brim of his mug, then he placed it on the counter and took a seat on one of the black leather bar stools. "I do remember where I put it. On the chest in our bedroom. I told you a hundred times." He glanced at me. "You haven't seen it anywhere, have you, Sam?"

Even if I'd walked past it, I sure hadn't paid attention. "Sorry, no. But I can help you look for it. Let me just shower off the stench of smoke and campfire, then we can sweep the house together."

Pamela appreciated my offer even though Uncle Jack looked at me skeptically. It was impossible to say what he was thinking, but he made me feel uncomfortable.

I hobbled to my room, grabbed fresh clothes, and took a welcome hot shower, taking care of my bandaged leg. By the time I stepped out of the stall, I realized how tired I really was.

Some sleep would be great. But first, I had to help my uncle find his watch, then maybe get a little drawing homework done. Hopefully I could have a nap after lunch—especially if I wanted to be a good sport at Lisa's sleepover tonight.

After toweling my hair dry, I gathered my clothes together with Tony's sweatshirt and dropped them into the laundry chute. Tony wouldn't want his hoodie back stinking like campfire.

As I walked out of the bathroom, Chloe came shuffling down the hall toward me on autopilot. She wore her silky pink dressing gown half-open, with her pink nightshirt flashing out underneath. Her hair was disheveled.

And freaking black.

"What the hell—" I stopped dead and stared at her, open-mouthed.

Chloe yawned, shoving strands of her newly dyed hair out of her eyes. "Get a grip, Samantha. It's just a color." She shoved past me into the bathroom and slammed the door shut.

Just a color? My ass. That was *my* hair color. She'd stolen it!

Chloe had always loathed black. She was a natural brunette—before she'd started to dye it blond. She'd hated dark hair all her life.

Rooted to the spot, I scratched my head. Who or what on earth had made her do that? Then again, it was none of my concern. Pushing the thought of my raven-haired cousin out of my mind, I went to find my uncle to help him search for his million-dollar watch. I heard him talking to my aunt in their bedroom and joined them. By now, Jack had changed into a pair of black trousers and a gray shirt. He looked presentable again as he pulled open one drawer after another in the chest opposite their bed, rummaging through each of them.

With her head in her hands, Pam sat at the edge of the king-sized bed. "Maybe you just thought you took it off because you do every day? We should start looking for it in the rest of the house."

Jack insisted he'd put his watch nowhere else than on top of the heavy wooden chest where Pam also kept her jewelry case and some pictures of Chloe. Together, we skimmed the room from top to bottom once more, but when that clearly got us nowhere, we proceeded into their bathroom, the hallway, the front room, the dining room, and the kitchen. If that Valentin or Constantin watch was still somewhere inside the house, it must have turned invisible.

We gave up after a couple of hours—Uncle Jack frustrated to the bone and me feeling sorry for my aunt, because he seemed to blame her for not taking enough care when the house had been cleaned yesterday.

I went back to my room and planted myself on the desk chair, ready for some drawing. I had finished most of the projects this week. Only one more to do.

The final drawing had to be of speed. Any kind of speed. It had only taken me a second to come up with a great idea when I had read the instructions on Monday and seen that Tony had sketched a rollercoaster. I actually couldn't wait to get started on it, because for my theme of speed, I chose a galloping horse.

I began outlining Lucifer's strong body, his long neck, flattened ears, and outstretched legs. In the end, though, something seemed wrong. I couldn't tell exactly what, but I assumed it must be his legs. Using the eraser, I first made subtle changes, then bigger changes, and finally I ripped the drawing paper from my pad, tossed it aside, and started from scratch.

Throughout the afternoon, I repeated the procedure three times, totally lost in my work. Until suddenly my cell phone went off next to me on the desk and tore me out of my concentration.

"Hey," I answered.

"Do you want me to pick you up?" Susan chirped into the speaker.

"What? What time is it?" Oh no. I had totally forgotten about Lisa and the sleepover.

"Six fifteen. We're supposed to be there in fifteen minutes. You don't sound ready to go."

"Umm..."

"*Why* don't you sound ready to go, Sam? You ain't gonna back out. I won't let you." She paused then continued in a not-so-demanding tone. "Unless your leg's giving you trouble. Ryan said this morning you had to see the vet. So...do you need surgery or something?"

What freaky film was running in Susan's head? Oh my God!

"No, Susan. I definitely don't need surgery. I just got caught up with homework. I'll be ready in ten minutes if that's fine with you."

"Fantastic. I'll honk when I get there." She paused then added with a conspiratorial note to her voice, "I'll park a little farther down the road. I don't want to be seen in front of Chloe's house again. People will start to think I'm friends with her."

"But you're friends with me. And I live here, too."

"Yeah. Right." Susan heaved a dramatic sigh. "I suppose I'll just have to get over that part. See you in ten."

When she hung up, I left my desk a mess of scrunched paper, pencils, eraser dirt, and a half-empty bottle of water. A sleepover. What did people take to one? I wondered while I packed my pajama shorts and a tank top. I scratched my head and turned on the spot. An additional pair of socks couldn't hurt. Really thick wool socks, so my feet wouldn't get cold in Lisa's room. And a blanket?

Crap. This was the first time I remembered Pamela's sleeping bag. I hadn't had a chance to bring it back home. My first thought was to go back to the campsite and fetch it. But that was a stupid idea. Susan would surely have packed it for me.

I slipped into my boots, slung the backpack over my shoulder, and walked downstairs to say goodbye to Aunt Pamela.

"Have fun, Sammy!" she shouted after me as a loud, double honk sounded outside and I walked out the door.

Mater's engine was still running when I climbed in, and Susan drove off even before I could close the door. I threw her an incredulous look, but she just shrugged. "Don't complain. I halted to let you get in. Is that nothing to you?"

Not staying a second too long in front of my family's

T is for...   157

house, I got it. I shook my head, out of comebacks to her lunacy, and buckled up.

As we arrived at the street where Tony lived, Susan halted in front of the next house, which looked rather identical. But instead of the small pool that I could spot now in Mitchell's yard, there was a shed in Lisa's. I grabbed my backpack from the floor, then hesitated to get out.

"Did you bring my sleeping bag?" I asked Susan in a hopeful tone.

"I don't have it. I had to carry so much this morning I just couldn't carry your stuff, too. Tony got it. He said he'd swing by later."

"I thought this was going to be a no-boys area tonight."

"It is. But you need something to sleep in, don't you?" Susan nodded for me to get out of the car. She locked her door and came around to lock mine, too, the ancient way—with the key actually sliding into the lock. "No worries, Sam," she said then. "I'm sure Tony knows how to behave around you by now. Anyway, I think you two got along pretty well last night. I mean with him lending you his hoodie and all."

And he'd driven me to the vet. "I'm not worried about him." Not anymore. "I just don't want to spoil our girls-only time. Maybe I should go grab it from Tony right now."

"He isn't home."

"How do you know?"

"Soccer practice until seven thirty. Chill, Sam. He'll give it to you when he gets home. And no one will mind."

All right, if she said so.

We walked up to Lisa's house and Susan entered without bothering to ring the bell. I, on the other hand, stopped on the doorstep, uncomfortable.

Susan grabbed the sleeve of my hoodie and pulled me inside. "Her parents aren't home tonight, and Lisa said we should just come up to her room. Loosen up. I think recently I've hung out more in this place than my own room. It's all cool."

I climbed the semi-winding stairs after Susan and followed her into a room to the left. Lisa, Allie, and Simone were already there and arguing over the first movie they wanted to watch tonight.

"Hey, everyone." I gave a quick wave toward where they sat on the bed.

Lisa jumped up and pulled my backpack from my shoulder. "Give me that and make yourself comfortable." She placed it on the swivel chair in front of her desk, which was overloaded with books and some other stuff. It could hardly be the place where she did her homework.

I glanced around the rest of the room and found I liked it. Untidy to the core, with clothes tossed over furniture, random items such as a hairbrush, a bottle of OJ, and DVD cases littered the carpeted floor. It looked more like home than any room in my cousin's house. A chest and wardrobe were placed against the wall with the door along with a hi-fi unit, and another shelf next to the desk held a widescreen TV.

Oh, Nicholas Hoult on *that* screen; I was so ready for it.

And I was lucky, Allie and Simone shared my enthusiasm

for the film. We all moved together so everyone could sit on the bed while we watched it after we put on our PJs. Allie, Lisa, and I were in boy shorts and tank tops, while Susan wore long flannel bottoms and a sweatshirt. Supermodel Simone had to outdo us all with her long, silvery satin nightgown.

We'd inhaled three boxes of pizza and Nicholas was about to sling his arms around Teresa Palmer when a whistle from outside caught our attention. "That's for you, Sam," Lisa said, not taking her eyes off the screen.

Neither did I, and I didn't understand what she meant anyway. "Huh?"

Now Lisa grabbed the remote for the DVD player and stopped Nicholas and Teresa mid-fall.

No—no! Don't stop it. The kiss... I wanted to see the kiss. *Ugh.*

But it was too late.

"Your sleeping bag has arrived." Lisa got out of bed and walked to the open window, leaning outside. "Hey, guys," she said, and I could hear her surprise.

"Are you girls all dressed?" came Ryan Hunter's voice, mischievous as always when he talked to his girlfriend.

"Yes. But you'd better not plan on coming up here." A rustling sound like a tree in the wind drifted inside and cut Lisa short for a moment. "That's against the rules," she said next with a playful sharpness. At the same time she backed away from the window and turned to us. "Sorry, girls. I hope it's okay with you if the guys come in for a moment?"

The guys? And come in *how*? I hugged my knees to my

chest, feeling a little uncomfortable wearing my pajamas in front of the boys.

"Is Sasha with them?" Allie whispered excitedly.

"I couldn't make him out in the dark," Lisa murmured. "There're many of them."

Ryan was the first to climb through the window. While he hugged Lisa from behind and kissed her temple, Tony, Nick, Alex, and even Sasha Torres followed. The room was suddenly crowded and filled with wild blabbering.

Tony came toward the bed and tossed a rolled-up red bundle at me. I caught Pam's sleeping bag and held it on my lap. "Thank you."

He nodded once, then his gaze landed on the bandage on my bare leg. "Sexy socks, Summers. How's that wound doing?"

I curled my toes. "No pain, no more limping. I guess I'm out of the woods."

He smiled then, and that smile was...wow...pretty enough to hold my attention for a silent couple of seconds.

"You know," Lisa told Tony from behind, "you could have dropped it on the doorstep. No need to bring half the soccer team up here to deliver it."

He turned around. Immediately, his smile widened to a lewd grin as he let his gaze move slowly up and down her body. "Blame your boyfriend, pretty girl. He was the one that showed up at my house ten minutes ago and dragged me over here."

I wasn't exactly sure why, but the corners of my mouth turned downward at that look on Tony's face. I couldn't help it, but I didn't like how he gaped at Lisa. And Ryan apparently didn't like it either.

"Back off, Mitchell," he warned Tony with a mocking note in his voice and hid Lisa behind his back. "She's mine."

Lisa giggled as she was shoved around by her boyfriend. She was probably used to the boys' bantering and Tony's coming on to her. I, however, wasn't. Holy crap, it gave my heart a twinge that hurt and annoyed me more than not being able to watch sexy Nick Hoult with my friends.

Too weird.

I climbed over Susan's legs, out of bed, and went to the bathroom. I'd been only half an hour ago, but I needed a minute to myself to sort this out. Where the heck had this uncomfortable feeling in my chest come from? I surely couldn't be jealous of Lisa. No freaking way. Not because of *Anthony Mitchell*.

I glared at myself in the mirror. "You. Suck."

Yeah, I did. When the hell had I grown feelings for stupid Mitchell? He was *not* my type. Or maybe he was, because I always fell for the blue-eyed blonds...

But tonight I refused to.

I squared my shoulders and swallowed the silly dryness in my throat. But when I went to walk out of the bathroom, I couldn't bring myself to open the door. I cringed, remembering that I was wearing boy shorts and stupid pink wool socks. Oh, the misery of it. Why couldn't I have brought freaking long pajamas like Susan tonight? Or even a silk gown like Simone. She definitely wasn't embarrassed in front of Alex wearing that.

I slumped with my back against the door. *Get a grip. Get.*

162   ANNA KATMORE

A. Grip! Now wasn't the time to panic. And I was probably mistaken anyway. I'd misinterpreted that twinge in my chest. Totally. No such thing as infatuation right here. I'd only been annoyed because Lisa had gotten all the attention in the room and I'd gotten none. Yeah, right, that must have been it.

Ha ha, my inner self laughed at me. *Like you've ever been a person to crave the attention in a room.*

I told my inner self where she could go with her laughing and aggressively pulled the bathroom door open. Biting down on my molars, I went back to Lisa's bedroom and found everyone sprawled out across the room: Susan and Allie still on the bed, Lisa in Ryan's lap on her swivel chair, Alex and Simone cuddling up on the floor, and Nick, Sasha, and Tony fighting over the remote for the hi-fi unit in the corner.

I assumed the girls' night was officially over. Great.

CHAPTER 11

I GRABBED MY sleeping bag, unrolled it at the foot of the bed, and sat down cross-legged. Before long Nick slumped down beside me.

"Hey, Finn Girl," he said and nudged my shoulder with his. "You sneaked off today and missed out on all the morning fun."

"Not intentionally. Ryan insisted on his father patching my leg up." I scrunched up my face. "I'd rather have stayed with you than have my leg burned out from the inside."

Someone dropped down on my other side and I was surprised to see it was Tony. Glad that I could look at his face and not feel like I needed to instantly kiss him, I relaxed. It *was* a mistake after all. No crazy attraction. *Phew*. I was safe.

"And you should have heard this little one swearing," he sold me out to Nick. "I promise you've never heard anything like it before." Tony leaned in and said in a lower voice to me, "From a girl's mouth, anyway."

A grin tugged at my lips. "You find that funny, do you? Me suffering?"

"Not at all." He bit his lip, trying a little too obviously not to smile. "I was totally suffering with you. You were such a poor little puppy, curling up on that table. I was afraid you'd nip me

164   ANNA KATMORE

any second." By the end of that, he was laughing so hard I felt the urge to shove a pillow down his throat.

Giggling, because his good mood was actually infectious, I gave him the best death glare I could manage under the circumstances. "I hate you."

Tony shrugged it off. "I don't care." But the warm look he gave me then said he *did* care. He knew I didn't mean it—anymore. And he seemed happy about it, which created a cozy feeling inside my chest. Way different from what I'd felt before.

Music came on and tore my attention away from Tony. It was a remix of some old Italian song. Sasha, who had won the fight over the remote, settled down on the floor next to us. After a few beats, he skipped to the next song and the next. He did it so many times that Susan finally lost her patience, leaned down from the bed, and snatched the remote from his hand. "If you guys want to stay," she warned them, "you go by our rules. We say what's going to happen."

"Ooh, and what *is* going to happen, book lover?" Ryan teased her, stroking Lisa's forearm up and down.

"Nick kissing Teresa. That's going to happen," I informed him and cast a grin over my shoulder at Susan. "Turn it on again."

"Me kissing who?" Nick asked then, totally confused but looking quite eager at the idea.

We all started to laugh and I told him, "Not you, silly. Nicholas Hoult. You guys came in before we could watch the best scene of the movie."

When Susan pressed play and Nicholas and Teresa

reemerged from the pool, Tony quirked his brows. "Ew, a movie kiss? This is what you girls do when you're by yourselves?"

"This is what we've been waiting for all week," I breathed, eyeing Tony. "So, in God's name, be quiet now."

He released an exasperated moan as he fell back against the bed, but I ignored him. Because at that moment, the other four girls and I were swooning over No-More-Zombie-Nick.

The only trouble was I suddenly wasn't seeing Nicholas and Teresa any longer, but imagined the couple on the screen to be Tony and me. With a start, I straightened and held my breath. *Shit.* Not what I wanted.

Scowling, I turned my head toward Tony and found him looking at me. I hadn't the slightest idea what he was thinking right then, but we stared at each other for a long, awkward moment. Slowly, he arched one questioning brow. I smiled and gave my head a little shake in confusion then turned away again.

Oh no, this was too weird. I needed to concentrate on something else or I would go crazy with that butterfly feeling on the rise in my stomach.

To me, it had been a given that if I ever fell for one of the guys, it would be Nick Frederickson, because he was a real cutie. But Tony? The one who had given me no break from the start? I couldn't—no I *wouldn't* have that.

I slumped back against the bed like the guys had and crossed my arms over my chest, glaring at the TV. Damn. I could feel it, Tony's eyes fixed on my face. My heart started to pound a little harder. *Please, please, stop*, I begged. *I don't want this.*

ANNA KATMORE

I didn't move a muscle until the movie was over, but as soon as it was, I rose from the floor and flopped onto the bed next to Susan. Anywhere was good, as long as it was away from Anthony Mitchell. "Boy, that kiss was hot," I exclaimed, fanning myself with an old birthday card from Lisa's night stand. Of course, it wasn't the kiss that had gotten me all hot and jumpy, but no one needed to know that.

"Yeah, *way* hot," Simone seconded me. "Anyone want ice cream? I think we need that now, Lisa."

"Agreed." Lisa got up from her boyfriend's lap, and we all followed her downstairs, where we gathered around the rectangular dining room table. She brought out a pack of wafer rolls and dished out bowls of strawberry and vanilla ice cream for everyone.

I had chosen a seat farthest away from Tony, just to be safe from myself. Still, every now and then I sneaked a glance over at him. He returned none of my looks. Not one. He was busy with his ice cream and talking to Alex about a new video game called GTA or something. I stopped looking at him then and let myself be dragged into an argument with the girls about which fictional creatures were the sexiest—vampires, werewolves, or demons.

As if there was even room for a discussion. "Vampires, of course," I declared. "Do none of you watch *The Vampire Diaries*?" If there was one guy in the world hotter than Nicholas Hoult it was Joseph Morgan. Blond hair, blue eyes...just *sa-woon*-worthy. But maybe that was only me.

"Vampires? Seriously, Summers? I thought you'd go more for the smaller creatures. Like one of the seven, you know,"

Tony said, and he totally startled me with a smirk.

I frowned at him. "The seven?"

"Dwarfs," he mouthed and winked at me.

I grabbed a wafer roll from the middle of the table and tossed it at Tony, who ducked out of the way before it hit his eye. It was amazing how he got away with mocking me for being tiny these days. But then, none of what he said now seemed or sounded in any way like an insult. I would have never guessed that I could actually enjoy his bantering. Even if he deserved a kick in the shin for it.

"So, which one's the sexiest, Summers? Sneezy or Dopey?"

Everyone laughed. Even me. But I couldn't let him off scot-free. "Come here, and I'll give you Dopey." I shot up from my seat and dashed around the table, but before I got to him, he'd risen, too, and escaped into the living room.

Tony jumped gracefully over the dark brown, L-shaped leather couch and used it as a barrier between us. I stopped beside the coffee table, glowering at him.

"What, you're scared of a tiny dwarf now?" I teased, then lurched forward over the couch, ignoring the slight pain in my leg. Tony was out of the way before my feet touched the floor again, and I spun around, finding him five feet away from me.

What was I doing here, chasing after Tony? He was bigger, he was leaner, he was faster, and I'd never catch him. Even if I did, what was I going to do to him? Wrestle him to the ground and force an apology out of his mouth? Well, at least it was an option...

He caught my hesitation, and the jerk actually started to

sing "Heigh-Ho." Before I knew it, I'd made one fast jump forward and knocked Tony over onto the couch, landing on his chest.

With his arms slung around me, he stared into my eyes, openly surprised. "Speedy," he said under his breath.

I wrestled my upper body free from his hold, but I couldn't do any damage like pinching or tickling, because he'd captured my wrists in an instant. I found myself in a very weird position, straddling Tony's hips, trying to get my fingers closer to tickle him.

"Now, what have you got planned, Summers?" He laughed at me. "It takes two of your size to actually overthrow me."

"I just *overthrew* you. And I'll get you eventually. You just wait." I put all my strength into my arms, but it was nowhere near enough. All it did was make Tony Mitchell laugh harder.

"Guys, I'm under dwarf attack!" He turned his head toward the entrance to the living room. "Can somebody help me, please?"

I clawed my fingers, but it did me no good. Tony's grip was gentle enough, yet firm. Like velvety iron.

Nick and Ryan came in then, and both bit down a chuckle when they saw me having a go at their friend. "Having a good time, guys?" Ryan asked, while Nick came forward and slung his arms around my body to lift me easily off Tony.

I shrieked, I laughed, and I choked. Then I lightheartedly cursed them all for sticking together against a single helpless little girl. Nick pressed my back against him, holding me prisoner, until Tony sat up and ran a hand through his hair.

"You'd better not fall asleep tonight, Mitchell, because I know where you live," I growled at him. The threat was forgotten the next instant when Nick's hand on my stomach surprised me as it homed in on my belly button.

"What the heck is that?" he blurted out. Without warning, he pushed my top upward to expose my belly and leaned over my shoulder to catch a glimpse.

I sucked in a breath and stepped away from him. "Excuse me?" But I couldn't push my tank top back down fast enough. He'd already seen my belly button piercing. I would have showed it to him if he'd asked, but pushing my top up in front of Tony and Ryan was hardly the way to go. I was lucky he hadn't shoved the top up any farther, because I didn't usually wear a bra underneath my PJs.

Tony tilted his head, seeming rather impressed. "Nice."

Nick topped that with, "Awesome. Did it hurt to get it done?"

It had. But compared to the pain of this morning, it had felt like a bug bite. I pressed my lips together and nodded once. In the meantime, Ryan grabbed the doorframe and leaned into the kitchen. "Baby, Sam has a belly button piercing."

"I know," Lisa answered. "I saw it at cheerleading the other day. Looks cool, huh?"

"Yeah. Can I get my eyebrow pierced now?"

"I don't think so."

"My lip?"

"Nope."

"A nipple?" He looked sweet as he waggled his eyebrows at

us.

"*No!*" came the resolute end to that conversation. It sounded like this was an argument the two of them had been having before tonight.

"Women," Ryan muttered with a frustrated pout and sat down on the other side of the couch. "They find everything cool as long as their boyfriends don't have it."

"I don't know." I shrugged and parked myself on the armrest of the couch, placing my feet on the seat. "I think I'd love my boyfriend to have a nipple piercing."

A smirk slipped onto Ryan's face then. "Baby—"

"No, Hunter!" Lisa cut him off. Then she came in and massaged his shoulders from behind. "I like your nipples the way they are. Clean and without bars in them."

Ryan snagged her wrist and pulled her over his shoulder, down onto his lap, making her giggle. He wrapped his arms around her, whispering something into her ear that made her blush and smile. She bit his earlobe next, and Ryan gave a playful growl. They were definitely the sweetest couple I knew.

Everyone found a seat on the couch then, except Alex and Simone, who made themselves comfortable on the carpet in front of the coffee table.

"What's your plan for the rest of the evening?" Ryan asked us girls, squinting around Lisa's head.

"I know," Tony said, "we could play strip poker...and remove your sexy socks, Summers." He hooked his index finger in my left sock and pulled gently as he smirked at me.

I slapped his hand away, but the sensation of his finger

skimming over the sensitive skin of my ankle stayed even after he'd removed his hand.

"It's supposed to be a movie night," Susan informed the guys. "Any wishes for what to watch next?"

Allie's suggestion was *Twilight*.

The boys immediately turned their thumbs down and made sick faces.

"Okay, then maybe *Titanic*?" Susan suggested.

"Oh come on, you don't expect us to watch sob stuff," Alex complained. Of course, the other guys backed him up.

"Excuse me, but it's not *your* night," Simone declared, sending her boyfriend a teasing look. "You're lucky we let you hang out with us and don't kick you out."

Holding on tighter to his girl, Alex rolled his eyes. "So can't we just find a compromise? Kissing *and* some action?"

We all silently deliberated. It wasn't actually that bad an idea.

"Which movie?" Lisa asked.

"Avatar?" Tony and I said simultaneously. I looked down at him and he smiled back.

Surprisingly enough, everyone was happy with that, and we agreed to stay downstairs, because there was more room for all of us on the couch. Lisa jogged upstairs to get the DVD. In the meantime, I slid down from the armrest and made myself comfortable next to Tony in the only free space left on the couch.

"God-awful taste in socks, but good taste in film, Summers," he told me in a low voice.

ANNA KATMORE

The fact that he wouldn't leave my socks alone made my cheeks grow warm. It was time for a confession. "I can't help it. I'm still cold in this unfamiliar climate."

"I can see that. You're sporting goose bumps." With the back of his knuckles, he rubbed my upper arm up and down once...and totally startled me out of my mind. Tony must have noticed my surprise. It obviously made him uncomfortable, because he pulled his hand away and cleared his throat, looking down at his fingers quickly and changing the subject. "So, how's the catching up for AVE going?"

"Not too bad. I've done four and started with the last today."

His gaze caught mine again, impressed. "You're fast. Which one's left?"

"Speed. I want to draw a racing horse." Remembering the trouble I'd had with it that afternoon, my forehead creased.

Tony, who caught my frown, demanded, "But?"

"But...it's hard for me to draw without live models. I guess I'll need a few more days to finish this one."

He seemed to consider my answer for a moment, but he said nothing more when Lisa put the DVD into the player, turned off the lights, and the film started.

Scooting lower in the couch, I stacked my feet like everyone else on the coffee table, while we watched two blue creatures getting personal. All this time, a cloud of the enticing scent of Tony's shower gel enveloped me. I took a few deep breaths, utterly relaxed, and soon realized that I should have taken that darn nap in the afternoon.

My eyes started to close for longer than just blinks. I had to fight to keep them open. Damn, the room was full of classmates. I couldn't just fall asleep next to them and be the weakest link. How embarrassing would that be? Especially with Tony sitting right next to me. What if I talked in my sleep?

What if I snored?

I had to stay awake and battle through the movie.

But the lack of sleep last night haunted me, and eventually I lost the fight.

*

There was a gentle tug at my hair. "Sam. It's time to wake up."

Tony's soft murmur dragged me sluggishly out of a dream about me turning blue and the president of the United States trying to catch me for a new freak zoo. I snapped my head up and bumped against something...hard. Pain seared through my skull.

Leaning back and opening my eyes for the first time, I rubbed the sore spot, trying to focus. I was half lying, half kneeling on the couch, my top had ridden up at my back, and there was moisture at the corner of my mouth.

Everyone was getting up and the girls were saying goodbye to their boyfriends. Only Tony remained on the couch next to me, feet still on the coffee table. He whined and clamped a hand over his mouth, squeezing his eyes shut.

I had no idea what was going on.

Eventually, he stuck a finger into his mouth and when he

pulled it out, there was blood on the tip. "Thanks for the head-butt. You just made me bite my tongue. And after I let you sleep away half the movie on my shoulder and drool on my shirt, too."

My gaze dropped to a wet spot on the green fabric of his shirt. Still dazed from sleep, I wiped my lips with the back of my hand. As the heat of shame crept to my cheeks, I croaked, "I'm sorry."

Tony grunted. I couldn't blame him for it. He rose from the couch and hurried after the others. "Guys, wait, I'm coming with you."

I waved at all the others when they said good night to me, then they slipped out the door. Tony was the only one who didn't turn to me. I heard him say goodbye to Lisa, and then he was gone, too.

It quickly grew quiet in the house. I was ready to walk upstairs and curl up in my sleeping bag. But suddenly I found myself the focal point of intrigued stares. "What?"

The girls cornered me, slumping down on the couch around me. "We haven't really had a chance to talk since last night," Simone cooed.

"We did," I countered. "We talked when Susan and I got here."

Allie Silverman flashed a wide grin. "We talked about your leg. But not about the obvious stuff."

"And that would be what?"

"You and Tony." Susan copied Allie's smile. "Things seem to have changed a lot between you two since the camping."

A queasy feeling ate at me. "Umm...maybe they have changed a little. No big deal, though."

"No big deal?" Lisa lifted her brows. "I only know of one other girl he ever let sleep on his chest."

Chest? I thought it was his shoulder. "He probably had no other choice when I tipped over."

"Believe me, if he wanted to, he would have had another choice."

Maybe Lisa was right. I was glad though, that Tony hadn't shoved me away like a nasty old dog with bad breath. That would have been even more embarrassing.

"Was it nice sleeping on his chest?" Susan demanded.

"I was asleep. How would I know?" Oh, for heaven's sake, could they stop pestering me now? Why did this feel like I was caught in crossfire?

"You know," Allie said in a low voice to Simone, "I think she's falling for him."

"You know," Simone replied, "I think you're right."

"Shove off, girls. I'm not falling for anybody. And it's really not fair to squeeze information out of someone who just woke up." I rose from the couch, waiting with an exasperated expression for them to follow me upstairs. It was two thirty in the morning. I yearned for sleep.

Fortunately, the girls took pity on me and we all went up to sleep in Lisa's bedroom. But two minutes after the light was turned off and everything was quiet, Lisa whispered, "Know what, Sam? I really think he likes you, too."

CHAPTER 12

I COULDN'T FALL asleep after Lisa's last words. Did she really think Tony liked me? If the rumors were to be believed, she was the one who knew him best, so if *she* said so, chances were she was right. But the other and far more important question was: Did I want him to like me?

I didn't answer that immediately, which made me a little nervous. What if the answer was yes? That would mean I was falling for Tony. Seriously—with no going back. It would complicate everything.

I refused to think about this for the entire night. At some point, I started to sing a silly song in my mind to silence my thoughts. Awkwardly enough, it was the dwarfs' "Heigh-Ho" I came up with. *Brilliant, Sam. Just bloody brilliant.* But it finally did the job, and I drifted off.

*

Morning with the girls was one of leisure, with a breakfast that dragged on until lunch. At least there was no more talk about Anthony Mitchell. This time we had a blast cornering Allie because of her cuddling up to Sasha during the movie last night.

Susan suggested we download a questionnaire from YourDatingServices.com to give to Sasha at school on Monday to see if he was a suitable match for Allie.

When I got my things together and Susan drove me home, it was already early afternoon. Jack greeted me in the hallway as I walked through the door. He seemed in a hurry, trying to slip into his shoes, put on his jacket, and fetch money from his wallet all at the same time.

He handed me two hundred-dollar bills that looked like they were fresh off the press. "Can you give this to your aunt when she gets home?" he asked me, shoving his wallet back into the inside pocket of his jacket. "I was called to an emergency meeting and won't be home until later tonight. The money is for Jab Jenkins."

"The gardener?"

"Yes. For extra hours. He'll come pick it up today. Pamela should be home by then."

He was almost out the door when I shouted after him, "Where's Pam?"

"Out for lunch with Jessie Hunter."

The door slammed shut behind him, and I was alone in a silent house. Well, almost. Chloe banged on the door to my room only a little later while I was practicing some dancing and demanded I turn down my music because she couldn't sleep out her hangover with noise like this.

I still couldn't get used to her raven-black hair, but I respected her wish. It was her home, not mine. Finding a more quiet distraction with drawing, I tried to finish that speed

ANNA KATMORE

picture. But it frustrated me more than yesterday, and finally I decided to give it a rest and make myself a sandwich instead.

Pam was already home and in the living room when I went downstairs. And look at that, the princess had risen from her beauty sleep, too. Chloe was watching TV while Pamela tried to fit new curtains to the wide windows. I pulled the two hundred dollars out of my pocket and passed them to my aunt together with the message from Uncle Jack.

My aunt pulled a face. "Jabbadiah called five minutes ago. His wife is ill and he won't make it today." She walked into the hall to find her purse and put the money away. "I'll give it to him later this week."

I shrugged, not really caring, and went to the fridge, loading food into my arms and carrying it to the counter. After I had eaten my turkey sandwich in the kitchen, I headed back to my room but halted in front of the stairs that led down to my uncle's gym. Though I had never done a workout down there, in the past Chloe and I had often played in the spacious room, pretending the fitness equipment was a pirate ship or a princess carriage. The walls were soundproof. And that gave me an idea.

"Pam?" I shouted over my shoulder, waiting until she stuck her head into the hall. "Do you think Jack would mind if I practiced dancing in the gym?"

"Of course not, dear. Go ahead." She smiled and disappeared into the living room once again.

I ran upstairs, changed into black cotton shorts, a top with spaghetti straps, and tennis shoes, grabbed my iPod, and rushed back down to the gym. On the way, I nicked a water bottle from the kitchen.

The gym was located just half a story beneath the ground floor, and since the land was on a slight gradient, they'd built a wall of windows overlooking the garden. Warm light flooded the room. I connected my music to the sound system lined up at one wall and moved some of the lighter equipment out of the way. With my hands placed on my hips, I glanced around the room.

Perfect. My very own dance studio.

I did some easy warm-up ballet, then skipped forward to a playlist of mostly Latin American songs with a strong, jumpy beat we'd used in my former Zumba class. Ely-T was my favorite singer from that list, and I chose a mix of aerobic and salsa dance elements. Sweat was beading everywhere on my body after only ten minutes. I loved it. This was one amazing way to lose myself. Music, if it was the right rhythm, moved me without my thinking about it. For a little while, it was only me and the beat.

I danced facing the window-wall and enjoyed the afternoon sun wrapping me up in light and warmth. My pulse was already raving from the workout. Crossing my legs, I spun on the spot.

And jumped back with a shriek, my hands clasped to my chest. "What the hell—"

Tony was leaning on the doorjamb, arms folded leisurely over his chest, his eyes dark with interest. For a crazy, long moment, I didn't move and music was all I heard.

How long had he been watching me? The uncomfortable warmth of embarrassment surged through my body. But given that my face was thoroughly wet and red from dancing, Tony probably didn't even catch my blush.

ANNA KATMORE

Eventually able to break eye contact, I walked over to the sound system and cut off the music. With a towel from the stack on the shelf, I wiped my face and cleavage, reining in my ragged breathing. "Who let you in?" I finally managed.

Tony didn't move away from the doorjamb, only his gaze followed me. "Chloe's mom."

"And that was *how* long ago?"

One corner of his mouth lifted in a smirk. "You should turn around more often when you dance."

Yeah, right. *Jerk.*

I drank from my water bottle, wandering to the other side of the room where I sat on one of Jack's weight benches, never taking my gaze off Tony. "So...?"

He adjusted the collar of his short-sleeved white shirt then shoved his hands into his jeans pockets. "So what?"

"So, is there a deeper meaning to your visit?"

At my harsh tone, his smirk disappeared and a frown pulled his eyebrows together. "Yeah well, I actually didn't come here to just watch TV with you."

"Oh, really?" What a shame. I might have enjoyed cuddling against his shoulder again. If I wasn't still in shock over seeing him in this house, of course. "Then what *was* your plan?"

Casually, Tony crossed the room and hooked one arm around Jack's propped up barbell. "Can you shower and then come with me for a while?"

"Why? Do I have another appointment with the vet?"

A smile played around the corners of his lips. "No. I want to show you something."

"Something?" I lifted one brow.

"Something cool. You'll like it."

"How would you know what I like?"

"Ah, I think I have an idea. Would you trust me now and get ready to go, please?"

"Cryptic *and* pushy." I took another swig of my drink. "Tell you what, I'll come if you tell me where we're going."

"Nah, I'm not saying. It's a surprise."

I didn't like how he grinned and stressed the last word, but he'd gotten me curious as hell. And frankly, the longer I stared at his bulging biceps where he'd slung his arm around the barbell, the more I wanted to go. Only, he didn't need to know that. "I don't like surprises," I told him flatly.

Tony's arm slipped away from the barbell and he came to stand in front of me. "Every girl loves surprises."

"I'm not *every girl.*"

"True, you're not." He said it so softly as he squatted down before me that the small hairs on my arms prickled. "We had a shitty start. I hurt you. Now I'm trying to make it up to you. Would you let me?"

"Um, I don't know." There was a cynical undertone in my voice, and the truth was, I really didn't know. Being with him yesterday morning had been like being with any of my other new friends. But looking at Tony now caused my heart to squeeze in a few extra beats. Things had changed so much over the past couple days that I didn't know what I wanted any longer.

As if he could read my mind, he cocked his head and lifted

ANNA KATMORE

his brows. "What are you scared of?"

"Nothing," I answered. Way too fast.

"Then come with me. And if it helps..." He straightened, holding one palm up and pressing the other to his chest as if he were in court. "I solemnly swear that I don't have any shit in mind."

I strangled a laugh by biting the inside of my cheek and heaved an overly exasperated sigh instead. "All right." Rising from the bench, I pointed a finger at his face. "But this better be worth it."

Without warning, Tony grabbed my wrist and pulled me to the door. "You can tell me later if it was. Now come. We're running late."

"Late for what?"

"You'll see." Then he added, "Bring your drawing stuff."

What? *Why? Gah!* This boy had to be the bastard son of *frustration.* I pulled my hand free to close the door as we left the gym, then we ascended the few steps together.

On the first floor, Chloe was just coming out of the living room. She stopped dead, her face suddenly ashen. I didn't know if it was appropriate to say something or just ignore her and walk upstairs to my room.

It was Tony who cut the silence, even if only with a murmur in my direction. "I'll wait outside."

"See you in a minute," I replied, remaining rooted to the top of the stairs.

Tony brushed past Chloe. I couldn't see his face, but the way Chloe's eyes moved to his, I guessed the two of them had locked gazes for the length of a breath. Then I heard him say in a cold voice, "Interesting change, Summers." He must have meant her hair.

When Tony was gone and I was alone with my cousin in the hallway, I got the full blast of her lethal scowl. "Are you crazy? Bringing Mit—"

"Excuse me, Chloe," I cut her off, "but I don't have time for this shit." I knew where this would go, and right then I preferred to get under the shower and ready to see Tony again instead of taking ridiculous jealousy crap from her. With one hand on the rail, I continued upstairs, taking them two at a time, and left her standing in the hallway.

In record time, I showered and slipped into the rusty red and brown camouflage pants that I had worn on my first night out in Grover Beach. It was warm enough, so I threw on a black T-shirt with a typed winking smiley face on the front.

Leaving the laces of my boots untied as usual, I quickly packed my sketchpad and some pencils into my backpack, then I sneaked out of my room, checking both sides of the hallway to make sure I wouldn't bump into Chloe again. She was nowhere in sight. Downstairs, however, Pamela caught me tiptoeing past the living room.

"That was Anthony Mitchell, right?" she said in a low voice.

I nodded.

"Things have changed between him and you then?"

I nodded again.

"That's great. I'm really happy for you, Sam."

"Chloe isn't. She'll hate me forever."

Pamela sighed, pursing her lips. "I'll talk to her about it."

"No, please don't," I begged my aunt quickly and took her hands. "She already thinks I'm trying to steal you from her. Let this be between her and me. We'll get this sorted out...somehow."

Pam looked at me as though she hadn't had any idea of what was going on between Chloe and me, but I knew she had noticed it from the start. "Okay."

"Thanks, Pam." Releasing her hands, I walked to the door.

Pamela walked with me. "Where are you two going?"

"I have no idea. He won't tell."

"Don't be home too late. It's a school night."

"I won't be." Hopefully. The truth was I had no idea when Tony intended to bring me back. With a wave over my shoulder, I walked outside and closed the door. There was no red car in the drive this time, but Tony sat on a metallic-green mountain bike, leaning his forearms on the handlebar.

"Do you have a bike?" he asked me. When I shook my head, he grimaced. "I guessed that. Unfortunately, I couldn't take my mom's car today, so you'll have to hop on here." He straightened and tapped at the handlebar.

My mouth fell open. "You're kidding me."

"It's a bit of a way. Too far to walk. So buck up, Summers, and get your butt up here." Tony smirked, reached over, and grabbed my hand, leaving me no choice as he dragged me forward. First he pulled my backpack from my shoulders to carry it himself. Otherwise it would only be in his way, he told me.

Steadying the bike then, he let me climb onto the handlebar, which wasn't as easy as they always made it look in movies. When I was sitting with my feet dangling but my hands anchored with an iron grip around the cold metal, he started to pedal, and we slowly moved down the street.

This was scary as hell, because soon we gained speed. A shaky whine escaped me.

"Relax. I've done this a hundred times." Tony's nose brushed my hair—or maybe it was my hair wafting into his face from the ride—as he said the soft words into my ear.

"*You* might have, but *I* haven't," I croaked. My palms started to sweat, giving me the feeling of losing my hold. "How far do we have to go?"

"Just out of town. About three miles."

Tony had to stand for the entire ten-minute ride, because I would have blocked his view if he sat. As the road turned slightly uphill and he had to step even harder into the pedals, he placed his forehead on my left shoulder, and I could not only hear his strained breathing but also feel it through the fabric of my shirt.

The lines of houses finally faded away at our sides, replaced by juicy green lowlands. A wonderfully fresh smell wafted around us, but I wondered what he wanted out here where there was nothing but grass, trees, and an occasional house every few hundred meters.

A white split-rail fence to our right hedged a wide area with a handful of horses in it. The dark animals were beautiful. I watched them grazing in the warm afternoon sun and didn't

ANNA KATMORE

notice that Tony had slowed down until we suddenly stopped at one corner of the fence. A trail led away from the road, following the pasture up to a nice little property.

"Get off. We have to walk from here," Tony told me. "The path is too bumpy for you on the handlebar."

I jumped off his bike and faced him with a questioning look. "Do you know the people who live here?"

"Yep."

"And we're going to visit them?"

"Not them. But the horses." Tony leaned his bike against the white fence and started walking toward the house. "You said you needed a live model. So... *Ta-da*." He sort of sang the last word as he spread his arms like he was presenting me with this paddock and the horses in it.

"I never thought I'd actually ever say this, but you're amazing, Anthony Mitchell." The urge to hug him rose within me, but I resisted and skipped ahead of him, whistling with two fingers to get the nearest horse's attention.

It was a gorgeous black stallion with one white hind leg and a blaze in the shape of a sword on its forehead. Tearing out a handful of grass near the fence and holding it out, I lured the animal closer. The stallion caught the grass between his lips then gave my shoulder a nudge that pushed me a couple of steps backward. He hadn't looked so tall from a distance.

"Who lives here?" I demanded, following Tony up the path and leaving the horse behind. "A friend of yours?"

"Not a friend. Family. And you know her."

"Her?" I frowned. How would I know any of his relatives?

But then it dawned on me. "Mrs. Jackson?"

"Yep. This is my aunt's land." His voice was a little strained. He climbed over an iron gate close to a nice white house with a dark gray roof and broad windows facing the paddock. "She's been breeding horses for as long as I can remember."

Unlike Tony, I didn't climb over, but ducked through the two metal bars parallel to the ground. "You sure she doesn't mind me coming here with you?"

Tony waited until I straightened again. "I called her this morning. She's happy to help you with your AVE project and thought it was a wonderful idea. Hopefully, it'll also help me get an A in her class this year."

That surprised me. "Your drawings are brilliant!" I bit my tongue and quickly corrected myself, trying to sound less enthusiastic. "Well, they're very nice, actually. She has no choice but to give you an A."

"Being my teacher *and* my aunt? You have no idea how hard she goes on me. It's totally unfair. Like I have to do everything three times as good as others just to get the same grades."

"She probably knows you have it in you and wants to coax it out that way. I think that's smart of her."

Tony cut me a stern glance as we approached the white house. "You wouldn't say that if she was *your* aunt." Then he rang the doorbell and we waited in front of the dark brown door to be welcomed.

Mrs. Jackson opened the door only half a minute later, her

ANNA KATMORE

smile widening when she saw us. Just like he had done with Jessie Hunter, Tony kissed his aunt on the cheek as he greeted her. It was lovely to watch him when he cared to show his good manners.

Mrs. Jackson then shook my hand. "Samantha. It's so nice to have you out here. Tony told me about your struggles with drawing a horse. I'm sure you'll find it easy with one of them in the paddock as a model."

I thanked her for the invitation and the opportunity, then I happily followed Tony across the yard to a romantic place behind the house.

An overburdened apple tree grew in the middle of a meadow next to the horses' pasture. Several fruits lay on the ground, but most of them still hung on the branches. I settled down in its shade with my back against the tree, breathing in the intense smell of leaves and fruit. Tony handed me my backpack with my drawing utensils. The sketchpad placed against my thighs and the pencil clasped tightly, I couldn't wait to get started. There was only one problem. "The horses are too far away."

Tony, who had just lain down in the soft grass, blinked at me. He knew what I wanted from him. "All right." With a groan, he jerked up again and strolled over to the fence. Using his fingers, he whistled so loudly that I flinched. Like I'd done before, he then ripped some grass from the ground and waved it at eye level of the nearest horse that had lifted its head at his signal. The brown animal stalked closer, ate the grass, then dipped its head and started grazing next to the fence.

Tony turned to me. "Happy?"

I gave him a sheepish look, shaking my head. "The black one?"

"Argh, Summers! Seriously?"

A smile curved my mouth.

"Fine." Rolling his eyes, he trudged away. A little later, he came back along the inside of the paddock's fence, leading the gorgeous stallion on a dark blue halter that the animal hadn't been wearing before. Tony obviously knew his way around this property and around the horses, too.

"I'm impressed," I admitted as he came and sat down beside me.

Tony raised his brows at my empty paper and taunted me, "You should be working."

Happy now, I started outlining the body of the horse with a few simple sketches, continuously looking up at the model. When the skeletal structure was finished, I began adding layer after layer, shaping the horse into a moving animal. But soon I faced a different problem.

Tony must have noticed my concern when I started chewing on my pencil instead of using it on the paper. "What's up?" he demanded.

"The horse isn't moving. I can't finish this if he stands still as a rock." I turned a pleading look to Tony. "Do you think you could make him move somehow?"

He shrugged and rose to his feet. "I can try." On the way over to the black stallion, he picked up an apple and then swayed it in front of the animal's mouth. When the horse

ANNA KATMORE

strained its neck to catch the fruit, Tony pulled his hand away and walked a few steps to the left. He climbed onto the split-rail fence and straddled the top. "Come here, horsey, horsey, horsey."

The stallion cocked his ears but otherwise didn't move.

"He isn't a cat," I told Tony, frowning at him in disbelief.

He grunted, hopped down, and walked back to the horse, teasing it with the fruit once more. "You want this yummy apple?" With a powerful thrust, he tossed it far out into the paddock. "Go get it!"

I giggled. "And he sure as hell isn't a dog!"

"Really, Miss Summers? Then tell me, what's *your* plan to improve this situation?" His voice was saccharin sweet.

I shrugged. "I don't know. Walk it?"

Tony heaved a sigh, deliberating. "You're insane, Summers." Nevertheless, he grabbed the blue halter and marched off with the stallion in tow. Boy and horse walked back and forth a few times while I made changes to my drawing.

"Faster!" I shouted.

Tony started to jog, the stallion trotting beside him.

I let them run for a few minutes, then tried again, "Think you can go a little faster?"

"No, I don't think I can, Sam," Tony gasped, letting go of the horse and bending over, hands braced on his knees. His hair a sweaty mess, he turned his face to me. His blue eyes shone in the bright light, his cheeks had turned red, and he bit his bottom lip. He looked gorgeous, just like that day when I'd gone to his house to get his notes.

T is for...

The corners of his mouth went up slightly which made me return a shy smile of my own.

And there I realized with shocking clarity that the girls had been right. I really *was* falling for this guy.

CHAPTER 13

TONY LEFT THE horse. As he made his way to me, he fished for his cell phone in his pocket and keyed in a number. "Hey... Samantha needs more action. Could you come out and run the horse? ... Okay." Tucking the cell back into his pocket, he grinned. "Plan B is in motion."

Plan B actually arrived three minutes later with a lunge line and a crop. Smiling, Mrs. Jackson asked me which horse she should train for my drawing. I pointed the black stallion out to her.

"Oh yes, Jostle is the pride of my breeding. Let's see if he's up for some activity today." She cinched the lunge line to his halter and led him away from the fence where the stallion had been rubbing his neck with pleasure.

After giving him a few minutes to get adjusted to the lunging, Mrs. Jackson had him trotting and then galloping in a wide circle. It was beautiful. The stallion moved gracefully, the power beneath his smooth, shiny coat visible.

"I don't think Carrie can make the horse run all day, so you'd better start drawing," Tony said as he sank to the grass next to me and broke my fascination with Jostle's fluid movements.

I pulled a lollipop from my pocket and, while sucking it, I started to finalize my picture with swift pencil strokes. Tony watched and sometimes gave me good advice. He had a fantastic eye for detail, light and shadow especially, and he made me correct every line that was misplaced, even by just a millimeter.

"You sound like you've drawn many horses in your life," I mumbled around the candy in my mouth.

"Some," he replied quietly. "When I was younger, I often came out here to draw. Carrie didn't mind. Some of my pictures still decorate the inside of her house."

"Did she also teach you how to put a halter on a horse?"

"Yeah. She wanted to give me riding lessons, too." He rolled his eyes. "I'm really not a horse person."

Concentrating on the left front leg and the accurate size of the hoof now, I squinted. "Riding lessons sound great. I would have loved to have my own horse."

"Carrie gives lessons for kids. My uncle died a long time ago. Now she takes in a bunch of kids every summer to teach them how to handle horses, and also to draw, if they're interested."

"Wow." I erased a misplaced stroke, wiped the rubber dust away with the back of my fingers, and blew on the picture to get it clean. "That's really nice of her."

Tony's shrug caught the corner of my eye. He crossed his arms behind his head and leaned against the tree trunk, gazing into the sun. "The house is big enough. Lisa and I stayed over often as well. She's afraid of riding, but she loved to groom the horses and braid their manes."

I hadn't expected him to mention Lisa in front of me, but since he had, I considered whether I could probe his relationship with her some more. "Susan said you're still in love with Lisa. Is it true?"

Even without looking up, I felt how Tony tensed beside me. I lifted my head and found him staring blankly at my face.

"Too personal, Summers."

Of course. I bit my lip and lowered my gaze back to my drawing, but his shocked expression haunted me. He thought I didn't know? Or did it bother him that I did? And what a stupid question it was, anyway. Like I hadn't known he was going to block it.

Like I had hoped he would say *no*...

Dream on, Sam. He's not interested in you.

Tony was nice to me now, and I should have been happy about it. There would never be anything more between us. Because even if his jibes had turned into a playful taunting, I wasn't his type. That simple.

Suppressing a sigh, I chewed on the smooth plastic lollipop stick. It was okay, I told myself. He didn't have to find me attractive or sweet or whatever. Because I wouldn't fall in love with him either. Mentally, I shrugged it off. It wasn't too late for me to get out of this. I'd just refuse to develop any stronger feelings for him.

Fortunately for me, my plan worked. I turned all my attention back to the project I had to finish. After a long moment, Tony continued telling me about his visits to his aunt's place. He didn't hold my getting too personal against me.

T is for...   195

"Right over there in the woods"—he nodded to my left—"is a place where we used to hang out a lot. When I came here alone, I often went there to draw the landscape. Only I turned it into a fairy woodland, with trolls and leprechauns peeking out from behind rocks, or little elves sitting on buttercups. I could get really imaginative there."

"That must be an awesome place." I looked at him sideways. "Would you mind showing me when we're done here?"

Tony nodded. "If the weather holds out."

Turning the other way, I saw the dark clouds he meant. They sneaked toward us, promising rain later today. Nothing to worry about. My drawing would be finished in a few minutes anyway.

A few more pencil strokes with Tony's instructions and soon I had a beautiful picture of a horse racing across a meadow, leaving rocks and bushes behind. It was perfect; the best drawing I had done in a long time.

"I have some great material on my computer about how to draw a body from the skeletal structure all the way to the last layer of skin. If you want, I can email it to you later," Tony offered as I added the date and my signature to the bottom of the picture.

"Sure." I ripped a small piece of paper from my sketchbook and scribbled my email address on it.

Tony arched one amused eyebrow as he read out loud, "Sammy-dot-Smrs? Does anyone really call you Sammy?"

"My mom does. And sometimes my aunt does, too." I put

the drawing into my folder and dropped it on the grass. Then I turned a provocative grin at him. "You don't think it fits me?"

A silent moment passed. He looked as though he wanted to say something silly like, "That's a name for a Golden Retriever". Luckily, he thought better of it. "Whatever I say now probably won't do me any good."

A giggle escaped me. "Nope, it certainly won't." After a while, a memory from the morning after camping resurfaced and I wanted to know, "Why did you call me Bungee yesterday?"

Tony took a deep breath. He stared me straight in the eye. Had I been too personal again? In just the moment I gave up hope of getting an answer, Tony opened his mouth, but Caroline Jackson broke him off shouting, "Samantha, if you're done with your picture, would you like to ride Jostle? I think he'd enjoy a little more exercise!"

My eyes widened at the offer. "I'd love to!"

"His bridle is in the stable, the first box on the right. You can go with or without saddle, up to you."

Was she kidding me? *Without!* I rose from the grass, dusting off my behind, then beamed down at Tony. "Are you okay if I go horseback riding for a bit? I mean, we're not in a hurry to get back, are we?"

"Not at all."

Without another word, I rushed into the stables and found Jostle's bridle in a metal box next to the wide rolling gate. As I spun, full of anticipation, I found Tony at the entrance. His hands had disappeared in his pockets as he leaned with one shoulder against the gate.

"Are you sure you want to do this?"

"Do what?" I asked.

"Ride that beast?"

"Yes. Why wouldn't I?"

It was hard to tell if he was trying to taunt me again or if he was really worried about me but then he let his smirk slip. "Because he's so big. And you're so...well..." His voice changed to a wry rumble. "You're tiny."

I laughed at that, but in an instant I had jumped onto the cube of pressed straw next to him, held onto the metal bars of the gate, and leaned into his face. "Look me in the eye and say that again," I teased with a growl.

Our noses almost rubbed against each other. The feeling I got then was weird. My heart sped up, my stomach felt like it was taking a ride in the washing machine, and my breath hitched. I knew this feeling. I'd had it last just before I'd been kissed for the first time.

Tony chuckled, disarming the situation. "Crazy little girl." He reached out for the reins in my hand and pulled me down from the cube, then out to the paddock again, as if I was his horse and he was my master.

A little disappointed, I followed him, but that feeling vanished as soon as Caroline Jackson had me bit Jostle and Tony came to help me onto the horse's back.

He held me by my ankle. "On three," he said, then counted quickly and catapulted me upward. Shading his eyes with his hand, he looked up at me. "Feel good?"

I nodded. Jostle's shoulders were level with the top of

Tony's head, but I wasn't afraid of horses, small or big ones. It had been years since I'd last sat on one, but surely riding was something you didn't forget.

Mrs. Jackson walked with me for a couple of minutes, but when she saw that I could handle Jostle well on my own, she removed the lunge line.

Tony went back to the apple tree and I tapped the stallion softly with my heels, spurring him on. The horse snorted and moved in long strides across the paddock. Reacting excellently to the light pressure of my legs, Jostle let me steer him in a wide circle, then a figure eight, and finally we galloped from one end to the other and back.

A few times I glanced over at Tony. He had grabbed my sketchpad and was idly doodling on it. I didn't mind. As long as he was occupied, I didn't have to worry my conscience for having fun while he had to wait for me. It wasn't long, though, before he seemed to grow bored of doodling and came over to the fence again. He sat on the top, placed his feet on the middle rung, and leaned his elbows on his thighs.

I reined Jostle in to a casual walk and rode toward Tony. His head turned from one side to the other as we passed him, locking gazes with me.

"Are you bored?" I asked him after another round, when Caroline had walked back to the house.

"A little," he confessed. "But you seem to be having the time of your life."

Smiling back over my shoulder as I was already ten meters away, I said more loudly, "At least the best time since I came back to Grover Beach." I nudged the stallion with my heels and raced him across the pasture once more, then I slowed him down in front of Tony and got ready to dismount.

I leaned forward and swung my leg over Jostle's back. When I slid down, strong hands grabbed me at either side of my waist and coaxed a gasp of surprise from me. Tony gently set me down on my feet.

I turned to him, the corners of my mouth lifting. "You think I'm too tiny to manage anything on my own, don't you?"

I was prepared for a mocking comeback, but not for his soft, intense look. "No. I just thought your leg might trouble you again if you jumped down."

Oh. I hadn't thought of that. "Thanks," I said, lower than before.

In the distance we heard the first rumble of thunder. It was still miles away, but it reminded me of the fairy tale woods he wanted to show me. "Do you think we can make it into the woods and back home before it starts to rain?"

"Possibly. If we follow the path through the woods, we'll get back to town from a different side. The distance is the same, so it doesn't matter which way we go."

Clasping Jostle's rein behind my back, I rocked back and forth on my heels, grinning. "Sounds like a plan."

After I had freed the stallion from the bridle and sent him back to his companions, we found Caroline inside and said goodbye. When she shook my hand, I told her thanks for giving me the chance to ride a horse again. She invited me to come back with Tony anytime I wanted, but I doubted that was going to happen.

While Tony got his bike, I fetched my backpack from under the apple tree. Then we strolled toward the woods behind Mrs. Jackson's property. The sky was darkening by the minute, but I didn't intend to stay much longer. I just wanted to see what inspired this boy.

About half a mile into the woods, Tony leaned his mountain bike against a chestnut tree. "We're going to climb up there." He pointed toward a rock face ahead. "If you're not carrying money in that bag, I suggest you leave it here."

Taking out my cell phone and tucking it into my pocket, I parked my backpack behind his front tire and followed him through the brush toward the rock face. Though it was steep and at least twenty feet high, Tony didn't hesitate to climb it. There were narrow crevices here and there and roots sprouting from cracks in the rock that one could grip for a better hold.

The lower half was obviously the easier part, and before going on, Tony waited for me on a small platform covered with moss and grass. He reached down and I took his hand, so he could haul me up to him.

With the momentum of the tug, I bumped into him, bracing myself against his chest. He steadied me with a gentle grip on my upper arms. His pecs twitched under my palms and he tilted his face down to me. I gazed into blue eyes that stood out against the gray rock face behind him. The same butterfly sensation I'd had in the stable returned with such impact that I felt like the ground was slipping away beneath my feet.

But this time something was different. Tony didn't defuse

the fire he ignited in me but seemed intent to fuel it with a single soft whisper. "Careful."

About what? About tripping...or getting too close and playing with fire?

The thunder rolling in the distance seemed to come closer, but neither of us cared. My heart banged against my rib cage, totally out of control. So much for refusing to fall for this guy.

I sucked my bottom lip between my teeth, then released it, breathing a little harder. Oh damn. Could he pull me that last inch toward him now and kiss me, please? I was aching for it.

Tony blinked. Once. Twice. Then he closed his eyes and a deep sigh escaped him.

No, he wasn't going to kiss me. Not now or ever...

TONY

SHE WAS ALL *Kiss me! Kiss me, Tony!* Frankly, I had no idea what stopped me. All I knew was that I took a deep breath, clenching my teeth, then I let go of Sam and took a small step back. As far as the wall of solid rock behind me allowed.

Her mouth fell open, and her dark brown eyes turned wide like those of the stallion she'd been riding before. Her nostrils flared slightly.

Fuck, I'd hurt her.

Again, a grumpy voice inside my head pointed out. Yeah, I could do that like no one else. What surprised me was that she would let me kiss her after all the crap that had been going on between us since the day of her arrival. One would think she'd shove me off the cliff the first chance she got.

But for a reason I couldn't explain to myself, she didn't. The girl just stood in front of me with sagging shoulders and an expression that tugged at my heart. *Ow.*

The good thing was, by now I knew how easily distracted Sam could get and I seized the chance. "Turn around," I told her as softly as possible without letting my frustration with my hesitation slip into my voice.

Her brows knitted together. "Hmm?"

I nodded at the landscape behind her without breaking eye contact, and this time she looked hesitantly over her shoulder. Then she spun around and gasped.

Mission accomplished. Samantha Summers was sucked into the beauty of the fascinating scenery before her and had forgotten all about me. Why did this make me ache to hold her again?

Pressing my back against the wall, I raked my hands through my hair and cut a scornful look skyward. This couldn't be true. I was attracted to Sam Summers. *Another* Summers out of all the girls in town. This was crazy. Shit, what was it about me and the women in her family that I couldn't keep my distance from them?

Sam half-turned back to me...and smiled.

Unfair! I wanted to scream at her.

"This is just beautiful," she breathed.

I pressed my lips together, forcing a tight smile, and lifted my brows quickly.

Sam gazed down at the multitude of trees, bushes, flowers, roots, and moss again. "It looks just like a page ripped out of a storybook. What an enchanting place." She was so immersed in the view that she didn't notice the first few drops of rain falling on her head. Only when the rain quickly got harder did she look up at the sky and wipe the drops away from her face. "I guess we missed our chance to get home dry."

Ten seconds later the sky opened its watergates and a downpour washed over us. Ducking her head, Sam shrieked and giggled at the same time. She was the only girl I knew who could do that and still sound lovely. With a wry expression on her face, she turned questioning eyes to me. "What do we do now?"

I grabbed her arm and pulled her toward me, then pointed at a tall crack in the rock face a few feet above us. "You get up there and hide in the cave," I said loudly enough for her to hear me over the pounding of the rain.

Helping her climb the first two steps, I made her move. But when I let go of her and jumped down from the ledge, she stopped, looked down at me, and shouted, "Where are *you* going?"

"To get your backpack!" With the rain coming down like this, her drawing would be ruined within minutes.

Little runs formed quickly at both sides of the path. I almost slipped on the soft ground. By the time I arrived at the tree where I had left my bike and Sam had left her bag, my shirt clung to me like a second, ugly wet skin. I strapped the dark red backpack over my shoulders and darted back to the rock face, scaling the wall toward the cave where Sam waited.

The hiding place was a narrow crack in the surface, barely broad enough for two. To get there, I had to climb a few steps higher, then jump to the surface where Sam stood. She had stepped back as far as she could, standing on a small rock. I reached her slightly out of breath and braced my impact with my palms at either side of her head. She gasped because I stopped mere inches before her face.

Water dripped from my hair down onto her sweet snub nose. A taunting drop wanted to be kissed away. Oh man, why did this girl tempt me so? She wasn't Lisa, I tried to argue with myself, but the cousin of the girl who was going to ruin my last years of high school with a lie. I couldn't trust Sam. Didn't want to.

But I wanted to fucking kiss those sensual lips in front of me.

Aware that I hadn't moved for the last half minute, only staring into Sam's big brown eyes, I dipped my chin a little. Just enough that the tip of my nose brushed that rain drop away from hers.

Sam's breathing sped up. Almost at eye level with her, I could feel it warm and soft on my chilled skin. Her hands touched my chest, uncertain and light.

"You shouldn't do this," she said, her voice a shaky whisper.

I shouldn't kiss her? "Why not?" Leaning in just a little more, I sounded gentler than I thought I could. Skimming the tip of my nose across Sam's cheekbone now, I closed my eyes and inhaled the fruity scent of her hair.

Her lips brushing against my cheek ignited a shiver down my back as she answered, "Because you don't really want it."

Two minutes ago I might have agreed. But right now I couldn't imagine anything I would rather do than kiss her. Just one short nip of that luscious bottom lip. Then I would pull back. And everything would be fine.

"Do *you* want it?" I breathed and placed a tender kiss on the soft spot behind her ear.

Sam stilled, then she sighed, slipping her fingers

ANNA KATMORE

underneath the straps of her backpack. "That doesn't matter."

"It matters to me."

"I can't seem to figure out what's going on inside your head."

"You don't have to."

"See, that's the problem," she almost whined. "You're confusing me. Everything you say seems to be at war with everything you do. This really is a bad idea." In spite of her words, she leaned into me, pressing her cheek against mine. God, who was the hypocrite now?

Her skin felt velvety soft, tempting me to nibble a path along her jaw. "You sound like you've never done anything stupid in your life," I whispered in her ear.

"Not like this. I think it would change too much...for *me*."

My palms still solidly placed against the rock behind her, I touched my brow to hers and looked her in the eye. "You think too much, Bungee." And with that, I was done talking. I tilted my head and brushed my lips against hers.

I took her bottom lip between my teeth and gently sucked. Sweeping my tongue across it, I could still taste the cherry lollipop and got lost in her soft moan.

Just one little kiss. Nothing was going to change. We would still be friends tomorrow. Not more. *Nothing. Would. Change.*

I took her hands in mine and moved them away from my chest, lacing my fingers through hers. Feeling her soft hands made me fully aware of how fragile and small she really was. A girl who needed to be protected...from idiots like me.

What the fuck was I doing? I didn't want a girlfriend.

Especially not Chloe's cousin.

Sam tasted wonderful, but I had to stop it now, or I wouldn't be able to in another moment. Just when she opened her mouth at my gentle demand and the tips of our tongues brushed against each other, I pulled back, struggling to catch my breath.

This. Was. *So*. Wrong.

To be continued...

Playlist

Nicki Minaj – Starships
(The Grover Beach Theme song)

Imagine Dragons – It's Time
(A rocky start)

Arash feat. Sean Paul – She Makes Me Go
(Someone's cheerleading...and someone's watching)

The Lumineers – Ho Hey
(Tony and Hunter playing soccer alone)

The Chordettes – Lollipop
(Declared to be the Sam Summers Theme song by Susan Miller)

Snow White – Heigh-Ho (The Dwarfs' Song)
(Tony is teasing Sam)

Ely-T – Bata Bata
(Sam dancing in the studio when she thinks she's alone)

A GROVER BEACH TEAM BOOK

S. ♡ T.
+

Kiss
with
cherry flavor

BESTSELLING AUTHOR
ANNA KATMORE

ANNA KATMORE

And so the story continues...

Samantha Summers finally got what she'd been secretly dreaming of since she came to Grover Beach. She'd been kissed by Tony Mitchell. But the next instant, he cops out and leaves her drowning in unrequited passion. An exhausting game of nearness and distance begins and threatens to drive Samantha crazy.

If that wasn't bad enough, chaos breaks loose in her current home. Things go missing, her cousin Chloe behaves more like a bitch than ever, mistrust grows in the family, and Sam is supposedly responsible for it all.

But how could she be when she did nothing wrong? And what can Tony do to fix it all?

KISS WITH CHERRY FLAVOR

At this place, I want to shout out my gratitude to

All my great readers for never letting me down. Your messages, your encouragement, and your friendships mean the world to me.

To my one and only *and absolutely awesome* critique partner, Georgia Lyn Hunter. I really wish we could meet one day, Lyn.

To my wonderful family for bearing with me in good and in bad times. I know it's not easy to live with a writer. Honestly, I *do* know.

ANNA KATMORE

ABOUT THE AUTHOR

ANNA KATMORE prefers blue to green, spring to winter, and writing to almost everything else. It helps her escape from a boring world to something with actual adventure and romance, she says. Even when she's not crafting a new story, you'll see her lounging with a book in some quiet spot. She was 17 when she left Vienna to live in the tranquil countryside of Austria, and from there she loves to plan trips with her family to anywhere in the world. Two of her favorite places? Disneyland and the deep dungeons of her creative mind.

For more information, please visit her website at www.annakatmore.com

Made in the USA
San Bernardino, CA
11 May 2015